Murder is as Easy as ABC

I0567723

an Ed Lazenby mystery

Charles Ray

Uhuru Press
North Potomac, MD

This is a work of fiction, and is not meant to represent any place, event, or person, and where the real thing is mentioned, it is in a fictionalized form only. Any similarities to real places, events or persons (living or dead) is purely coincidental.

The reproduction or distribution, by any means, including electronic distribution, is expressly prohibited without the written consent of the copyright holder, except for fair use quotes in connection with reviews.

For information about this and other works of this author, contact the author at charlesray.author@gmail.com.

Printed in the United States of America

Cover design by the author.

DEDICATION

To the overworked and underpaid teachers, who labor to prepare the younger generations to survive in an increasingly hostile environment.

CHAPTER 1

She stood with her shoulders back and her hands placed defiantly on her narrow hips. Her bright blue eyes blazed, and full, naturally red lips stuck out in an angry pout. Despite the serious expression on her face, and the angry red flaming circles on her cheeks, he had to fight to keep from smiling, because the smudges of red and yellow paint on her light blue jump suit were so not in keeping with the anger she was projecting across the space that separated them.

"You're a grouchy old man, and I hate you," the little girl said, jerking her head and causing her pigtails to sway back and forth across her face, which had looked cherubic when he'd seen her smile, but now made her look like an imp from hell. Ed looked down at her, the expression on his brown face as passive as he could manage under the circumstances.

"I am not old," he said.

"Are too," she shot back. "You look older than my grandfather, and he's *real* old, probably fifty or sixty."

Darn, he thought, I guess to her I *am* old.

"Well, I'm not grouchy."

"You are so. You're the grouchiest person I've ever met, and you're mean too."

Ed sat back in the uncomfortably small chair and looked at his inquisitor. To say that he was taken aback by her brazenness would have been an understatement. He was flummoxed. In his day, which was, admittedly, eons in the past, such behavior by a mere child toward a grownup, especially one who had just celebrated his seventieth birthday as he had two days earlier, would've earned a quick and painful trip to the woodshed, or at school, to being bent over a desk so that a teacher could administer several swipes with a switch or a wooden ruler. Not these days, though, oh no. Touch a student without said student's permission, and you were fired—if you were lucky. And, you were only allowed to touch to adjust an article of clothing such as a windbreaker or sweater, or to help a younger student put on his or her shoes You could end up in court or jail for assault if you touched anything else, or so they'd been told at the orientation session. School had really changed in the years since he'd graduated.

He took a deep breath, and tried to collect his thoughts, his mind wandering back to how this confrontation had started.

* * *

He and his neighbor and best friend, Ernesto Cardoza, had been sitting on his back patio, sipping *Dos Equis* beer directly from the bottle, and enjoying the balmy spring weather, when the Wertheim sisters,

Violet and Rose, had appeared from around the corner of his house. If he hadn't been on his second beer, he would've noticed the suspicious gleam in Rose's eyes, wouldn't have been caught off guard, and things would've worked out differently.

"Hi, guys," Rose said, with a cheerier-than-usual tone in her voice.

Violet just grunted, which was her normal way of greeting friends. People she didn't like didn't even get a grunt from her.

"Hi, Rose," Ernesto said, toasting her with his beer bottle, causing the wedge of lime he'd stuffed down the neck to bob up and down. "What're you gals up to?"

Violet sniffed. Rose smiled. "Oh, we were just out for a walk, enjoying the nice weather, and thought we'd drop by and see what you two were up to," she said. Violet sniffed again.

The beer kept Ed from noticing the sharp-eyed glances Violet kept shooting at her younger sister.

"Why don't you pull up a chair and join us," he said. "We've got plenty of beer left—I think. And, if you don't want beer, I have a bottle of white wine in the fridge."

The two sisters hurried over. They each grabbed one of the empty wicker chairs arranged around the wicker table, which was the sum total of Ed's patio furniture, except for the green charcoal grill that was beginning to show as much brown rust as green paint from being left outside so long. Rose, as she usually did, moved her chair around to sit next to Ernesto, who was now staring dreamily at her over the top of his bottle, and who had a loopy smile on his face. Violet clomped her chair down across the table from

Ed and dropped in it as if she was tired from a long hike. She reached up with a bony hand and brushed at a stray lock of bright red hair that had slipped out of the severe, combed-back hair style she'd taken to wearing of late.

"I'll have one of those beers," she said.

"I normally prefer white wine," Rose said, pushing a lock of her light blue hair from in front of her light blue eyes and giving Ernesto an eye-lash-fluttering look. "But, since everyone else is drinking beer, I guess I'll have that too."

Ed leaned over and retrieved two bottles from the ice chest on the flagstones between him and Ernesto, and placed them on the table.

"Well, aren't you going to open them?" Violet asked.

"They're screw caps," he said. "You just twist 'em off."

"When I give you a drink at my house, I uncap and pour it," she said, sniffing again.

"Oh, Violet, it's okay," Rose said. "It's really no trouble to remove the cap. Even I can do it." To illustrate her point, Rose deftly unscrewed the cap, dropped it on the table, and took a sip of beer, spilling a few drops on her chin as she did so.

Ernesto reached over and wiped her chin.

"You spilled a little," he said.

"Why, thank you, kind sir."

Ed rolled his eyes.

"Give it a rest, you two," Violet said. "Or, get a room."

Rose's cheeks turned as red as her namesake flower. Ernesto smiled guiltily.

"Violet, please," Rose said.

"Good grief. I'm so tired of you two tippy-toeing around like a couple of love-sick puppies. Either start acting like two grownups who happen to like each other, or cut it out."

Ed, even though he thought Violet was being unnecessarily harsh—something she was prone to do even at the best of times—didn't disagree with her sentiment. He found Ernesto and Rose's efforts to conceal the way they felt about each other from everyone else, while everyone else saw it as plainly as if it had been broadcast on an interstate billboard, embarrassing, as embarrassing as watching reality TV.

As a consequence, when Ernesto gave him a 'help me out here' look, he said, "I think Violet's being a bit rough on your guys, but she's right, you know. If you think no one knows that you two are an item, you're the only two people here in PVC who believes that. You should just own up to it and enjoy each other's company a bit more."

"Thanks, amigo," Ernesto said. "I thought you were on my side."

"I am, Ernesto, I am. But, you two aren't fooling anyone with your playacting."

"Really?"

"Really, man. I doubt there's anyone here in Potomac Valley Community who moved in before yesterday who doesn't know you two have a thing for each other."

Ernesto looked at Rose.

"You know, Rosie, he has a point. Maybe we should—"

"I was thinking the same thing," Rose said.

"So, I can hold your hand when we walk to supper

5

at the community center?"

She smiled coyly. "You can do more than that."

Violet snorted, a really loud snort. "Oh, please," she said. "That's worse than you trying to pretend you don't have the hots for each other. You're going to make me upchuck my beer."

Ernesto was looking like a fish that's just been pulled from the water and dumped in the bottom of the boat. His eyes were bugged wide, and his mouth was opening and closing as if he was struggling for air. Ed felt sorry for him.

"C'mon, Violet," he said. "Give 'em a break. I imagine it's been a while for both of 'em, you know."

"Yeah, my little sister has been a dry well for a long time." Violet laughed at her own lame joke, and when everyone else looked shocked, laughed even harder. "Okay, okay," she said finally. "I'll leave you two love birds alone. Besides, Rose, we need to do what we came for and hit a few more houses before supper."

Little bells went off in Ed's head, but he couldn't be sure it wasn't the effects of nearly two beers, so he ignored them.

"What's that?" Ernesto asked.

Rose laid her hand on his. He flinched like he'd been burned, but didn't move his hand.

"Well," she said. "Violet and I have this little project that we're looking for volunteers to help us with."

"What kind of project?" Ed asked. "This doesn't have anything to do with Vickers' request last week that the residents of PVC get involved in community service projects, does it?"

Vickers was Dr. Roland Vickers, CEO and resident physician for the Potomac Valley Community, a retirement community of condos and small cottages on Norbeck Road, just east of Georgia Avenue in Rockville, Maryland. A died in the wool bureaucrat who was always looking for ways to burnish his credentials for the community's board of directors, he never ceased to come up with some project to show what an innovative CEO he was—always through the actions of others. The way Rose frowned at his question, he knew her 'project' was in fact related to Vickers' request that the residents do something to show their neighbors that they were productive members of the larger community.

"Uh, well, yes, it is," Rose said. "But, this is a great project; one that benefits everyone involved. I think you'd love it. In fact, I *know* you will. The two of you would be perfect for it."

Ernesto was only paying half attention to what she was saying, he was so preoccupied with her hand holding his.

"What is this great project, Rosie?"

"You tell them, Violet. You're much better at this than I am."

That, Ed could agree with. Rose would take thirty minutes explaining all the good points of the project before even naming it. whereas Violet, never one to waste words, would tell you what she wanted you to do without bothering to tell you why it was important that you do it.

"Yes, Violet," Ed said. "Please tell us what it is."

She shot him a calculating look. Again, his usual sense of danger should've warned him, and didn't—not until it was too late.

"Like Violet said, it's a very important project. One

that improves the future for this community, and as a veteran and former government worker, it would be right up your alley."

Ed tried to imagine what it could be, missing the fact that, for once, Violet hadn't come straight to the point. That caused him to make a mistake.

"Sounds interesting. What would you want me, er, us to do?"

She smiled. "Good. I knew you'd volunteer. Our project is tutoring at-risk kids who attend Vernon Heights Middle School. I figured the two of you, with your background working in government, could tutor on civics and reading. We start Monday morning at 9:30. It's not much of a burden; we only have to be there until 11:00."

Her words slowly penetrated Ed's consciousness: tutor, kids, middle school, thanks for volunteering. *Oh, my goodness, what have I just allowed myself to be talked into?* The fact that he hadn't really said he'd do it, but had implied that he was interested, left him in a major bind. If he now said no, he would irritate and disappoint two of his small circle of friends, and he didn't want to do that. But, he'd never been good with kids, and kids of the middle-school-age were, in his opinion, worse than two-year-old children going through their rebellious phase. At least a two-year-old had the excuse of not knowing better. Kids in their early teens *knew* better, knew full well that they were rubbing your nerves raw, and did it anyway.

He sighed. An hour and a half didn't seem like too much of a strain. Then, he thought to ask an important question, "Is this an hour and a half, five days a week?"

"No, just three. Monday, Wednesday, and Friday. A piece of cake," Violet said. "It won't even interfere with your weekly golf game."

* * *

And, that was how he found himself facing off with thirteen-year-old Shirley Kent, in art class, arguing over the color of the apples she'd done for the assignment, which she'd colored purple, and had thrown a tantrum when Ed said that they should be red, green, or even yellow, but that apples were *not* purple.

It was Wednesday, his second day of volunteering, and he'd let himself be talked into tutoring the art class which ran from 9:30 to 10:30. The regular teacher had called in sick, and the principal, Douglas Southeby, a thin, sour-looking man with the beginnings of a paunch, stooped shoulders, and an ineffective comb-over that failed to conceal the fact that his hairline had receded to the top of his narrow skull, had asked if Ed could fill in, because he didn't have time to get a substitute teacher. The man had welcomed the volunteer tutors, and after only a day was treating them with the same officious disdain as the regular teaching staff. He reminded Ed of a number of bureaucrats he'd had to endure when he worked as a systems analyst at the Pentagon after leaving the army. As a result, he hated his guts. But, he'd given his word, and Ed Lazenby wasn't one to go back on his word, so he agreed.

"I'm sorry, Shirley," he said. "I wasn't trying to be mean. I just said that apples aren't purple. Now, if

9

you'd painted grapes, purple would be the appropriate color."

She stamped her foot, her penny loafers making a sharp cracking sound on the tile floors.

"It's my painting. Things can be any color I want them to be, and I want my apples to be violet. It's violet, by the way, not purple."

Ed knew when he was in a no-win situation. He also knew that she was right. It *was* her picture, and the students *were* supposed to be exercising creativity, so, if she wanted to paint purple apples, well then, purple apples it was.

"You're absolutely right," he said. "You can make them any color you want. I apologize for my lack of artistic sensibility. Actually, it's quite nice, now that I look at it longer."

She looked at him suspiciously, with that expression teens have when they're not sure if an adult is taking them seriously or shining them on. Then, she smiled, obviously deciding that he was being sincere.

"Okay. I'm sorry I called you mean. But, you shouldn't insult a person's art, you know."

Ed nodded. "Absolutely, and thank you for reminding me that art is in the eye of the beholder. It won't happen again."

With a triumphant smile, she tucked the still slightly damp acrylic painting under her arm, smearing more paint on her jump suit, and went back to her desk.

Dang right, it won't happen again. If Southeby asks me to do anything other than civics or reading, I'll say no, and if he insists, I'll pop him on that hawk beak of his. Hell, it's not like he can fire me or anything, since I'm doing this for free.

Charles Ray

CHAPTER 2

Ed glanced at his watch. It was 10:26; four minutes until his reading tutoring session with little Joseph Garcia. He stood and stretched.

"Okay, ladies and gentlemen," he said. "It's been fun, but it's time for your next class. Have a nice day."

He heard them tittering and giggling as he left the classroom, as relieved to be getting away from them as, he was sure, they were that he was leaving. He actually enjoyed his sessions with Joseph, though. The lad was small for thirteen, and painfully shy, partly because of his inability to read, and partly because he was much smaller than the other boys of the same age. Ed had been assigned to help him find a way to improve his reading skills; a task he looked forward to, for he was convinced that anyone could learn to read given the proper stimulation and motivation.

The boy appeared motivated to learn to read, but Ed had spent the entire session on Monday trying to find a way teach him to recognize and remember words, to no avail. About halfway through the session, though, he realized that the boy was not slow, he was, in fact, quite bright. He just couldn't recognize printed words.

As usual, Joseph was waiting for him when he arrived at the little anteroom off the library that Southeby had ordered set aside for the sessions. In his khaki pants and brown and white striped polo shirt, his scrubbed-shiny brown face alight with a broad smile as Ed entered, he looked more like a happy nine- or ten-year-old than thirteen.

"Good morning, Mr. Ed," he said, which caused Ed to giggle, because it reminded him of an old black and white TV show about a talking horse named 'Mister Ed,' but, of course, Joseph didn't have a clue what he was talking about it when he'd explained on Monday why he laughed.

"Good morning, Joseph. How are you today?"

"I'm fine."

"Did you try the exercise I showed you on Monday?"

Joseph's light brown cheeks darkened. "Uh, yeah, but there was nobody at home to help me do it."

Ed understood that. Jorge Garcia, Joseph's father, was a Salvadorian immigrant who worked for a lawn service country. His English was passable, but, having only finished high school in his home country, he didn't possess the skills to help his son. The boy's mother, Maria, who had followed her husband to America by two years, hadn't even been able to attend school in El Salvador, and was barely able to read Spanish, and spoke only a few words of English. The boy had been born the year after his mother arrived in Rockville, and, living in a Spanish-speaking household, in a neighborhood that was predominantly Hispanic immigrants, but attending schools that were a hodge-podge of nationalities, was perfectly bilingual—he just couldn't read very well.

After his first session on Monday, Ed had cancelled his planned golf with Ernesto and gone to the Rockville Public Library, where he spent the entire afternoon reading everything he could find on the helping children learn to read. That's where he learned about a condition called dyslexia.

Dyslexia, though it affects 20 percent of school-age children in the United States, is not completely understood. While it's known that it's a condition that causes people—even adults, and about 40 million of them in the US are affected—to be unable to match sounds to their written symbols, remember words by sight, or name sequences of letters, words, or symbols, what causes it, or precisely how to treat it is not clear. Some people incorrectly associate it with mental retardation or other emotional illness, and some scientists think it might be an inheritable condition. What seemed clear to Ed, though, was that most reputable scientists agreed that it was not a condition that could be successfully treated with therapy or drugs, only through using innovative teaching methods, because it could only be mitigated, not cured or eradicated.

In the US, schools were required to establish individual education programs for children diagnosed as dyslexic. The problem with that was that probably only five percent ever were. The rest were treated as slow learners, and often held back in grades, which further reinforced the belief that they just lacked intelligence, because repeating a grade still didn't help them learn to read.

Joseph Garcia had been one of the unlucky ones, by living in a district where the school to which his residence assigned him was led by one of the most unimaginative bureaucrats one could ever imagine, and staffed by overworked, underpaid teachers who only wanted the final bell to ring each day, and who seemed not to care much about their students beyond them successfully passing the required standardized tests. Unfortunately, Joseph, even though he did well enough on the math and non-reading tests, always bombed the reading comprehension tests. By fourth grade the teachers had given up on him, and his parents hadn't thought to have him tested—or, were too poor to afford the test—Ed wasn't sure which. He would've had it done himself, but the law required that a parent or guardian, or a member of the school teaching staff request such testing, something bureaucrat Douglas Southeby had neglected, or refused, to do.

Southeby had told Ed that first day that if he was unable to raise Joseph's reading score on the standardized test by the end of the school year, a mere three weeks away, the boy would be held back a year. Ed's reading had informed him that not only would this not result in any improvement, but would further damage what little self-esteem Joseph had left. He was determined not to fail.

"No problem, Joseph," he said. "Yesterday, I came up with an idea that I think will help you, and it's one you can do all by yourself."

The boy's face brightened.

"Really? Is it easier than me having to read a book where I don't know half the words?"

Ed laughed. "Much easier, I promise." He reached into his thin attaché case and withdrew a deck of large cards. He'd spent most of Tuesday cutting the white cardboard he'd purchased from the CVS Pharmacy, and making the drawings and letters, done with a colored pen set purchased at the same time.

He put the cards on the desk between them and began spreading them out. On each was a crude drawing along with a neatly-lettered word. An apple, red instead of purple, with the word APPLE underneath. He'd reasoned that helping Joseph associate the word with a concrete picture would help him learn to read. He'd seen at least two articles recommending flash cards.

Joseph reached out and picked up the APPLE card. He stared at it for a moment. "This word is apple, right?" He looked at Ed with hope in his brown eyes.

"That's right, absolutely right." His heart beat faster. "Each card has a picture; I'm sorry I'm not a very good artist, but these will do for starters, and we'll get better cards later; and the word describing or naming that picture. You look at the picture, and you say the word. And, the nice thing is, you don't need anyone to help you."

"Wow, can we try it now?"

"Of course, we can, Joseph," Ed said. "Now, you just relax, and I'll show you a card. Take your time, and see if you can tell me the word that's on that card. Okay?"

"Okay, let's do it."

Ed began slowly, turning cards over one at a time, starting with what he felt would be easy ones. The first one was a crudely-drawn evergreen with the word

17

TREE beneath it. Joseph looked at the picture, and looked longer at the word, his brow furrowed in concentration. Then, he smiled.

"Tree," he said, smiling hopefully at Ed.

"Right. That's a bad picture, but it's a tree. Now, get that picture in your mind along with the word underneath it. The next time you see the word 'tree,' think of that picture and say the word."

"Another one."

The next picture was Ed's idea of a fresh-baked loaf of bread in a pan. Underneath the picture he'd written, BREAD. This one seemed to puzzle Joseph. He put his finger on the picture, first on the brown part that represented bread, and then on the blue-gray pan, as if undecided which the word represented. Then, he validated Ed's opinion that he was a really smart kid.

"Bread," he said. "It's bread, right?"

"It is. You were unsure at first, though, weren't you?"

"Well, I thought it might be the pan, because you drew it better, but then, I figured if the word was pan, it wouldn't have bread, so I guessed bread."

Ed reached over and patted his shoulder. "You did more than just guess, young man," he said. "You went through a process of analysis and reasoning, and came to the correct conclusion. I know a lot of adults who can't do that."

"Does that mean I'm not a dummy, Mr. Ed?"

Ed knew where that question came from. Kids of all ages can be extremely cruel, and Ed was sure the teachers treated Joseph as if he was not too smart, which would make him a target for name calling and teasing.

"You, Joseph Garcia, are definitely *not* a dummy. In fact, you're one of the smartest kids I know."

Joseph frowned. "If I'm so smart, why are they telling me I have to repeat seventh grade?"

"Who the he-, er, I mean, where did you hear that?"

"I heard my teacher, Miss Wheeler, talking to the principal, and he was telling her I would be held back if I didn't pass the reading test this month."

Ed's cheeks felt hot. The nerve of those two, discussing a student where they could be overheard, and worse, by the student they were discussing. He bit back a quick retort to keep from accidentally allowing a profanity to slip in, and before he could respond, a noise behind him distracted him.

He turned to see the school janitor, Thomas Hadley, pushing a large box through the door. The man looked surprised to find the room occupied. He stood, wiping his meaty hands on his overalls.

"Uh, 'scuse me," he said. "Didn't know this room was bein' used. I'll come back later."

Ed held up a hand as he started backing through the door.

"Oh, that's okay," he said. "We're almost done with this session. Does what you have to do involve much noise?"

"No, hardly none at all. I just have to restock the library supply cabinet. They got in a new shipment of card stock, glue and such."

"Well, in that case, go right ahead. You won't bother us."

Hadley smiled, ducked his head, and began pushing the big box toward the row of cabinets opposite where Ed and Joseph sat. Except for the ripping sound as he yanked the shipping tape off the box, the only sound he made was his out of tune, barely audible humming as he began pulling items from the box and putting them on the shelves inside the cabinets.

Ed turned back to Joseph. "Now, we're going to do some hard ones. Are you ready?" He'd decided that it was best not to talk about the possibility of Joseph being held back.

Joseph tried to put on a brave face, but Ed could see the uncertainty in his eyes. He shuffled through the cards, finally settling on COW, only because the drawing for the one that said HORSE looked like a brown cow without horns. He turned the card over and put it in the center of the table.

"Oh, that's easy," Joseph said. "That's cow. You drew the cow good."

"It's you drew the cow *well*, Joseph." *But, please don't ask me why, because, for the life of me, I can never remember the reason.*

"Right, you drew the cow well," Joseph said. "It's a real *good* cow." He winked, and they both laughed.

Ignoring the janitor, they worked their way through the deck of cards, laughing harder and harder as Joseph critiqued Ed's artwork with each correct answer, and gave the Spanish word, which Ed didn't know, for those pictures he either didn't know the English word for, or because they were so crudely drawn, he didn't recognize what they were. They were so engrossed in the exercise, they didn't notice when Bradley stopped working and turned to watch them, a grandfatherly smile on his craggy face, or when his smile turned to a frown when Douglas Southeby opened the door and entered the room, his normally sour expression turning dark when he heard them laughing. It was only the strident sound of his nasally voice that got their attention.

"And, just what is going on here?" he asked. "This is supposed to be a learning session, not comedy time."

Ed dropped the card he was holding and twisted around in his chair. Joseph looked up and past Ed, a stricken look on his face.

"Oh, Principal Southeby," Ed said. "Joseph and I were just trying a new method to help him learn to recognize words."

Southeby stalked across the room and stood looking down his nose at Ed.

"Tutoring is supposed to be a serious undertaking, Mr. Lazenby. It appeared to me that the two of you were merely playing a game."

"Well, it is a game, but one designed to help Joseph recognize words by associating them with the object. It's supposed to be helpful for kids with dyslexia."

"Dyslexia? And, just what makes you think this young man is dyslexic? Are you a trained therapist or counselor?"

"Uh, no," Ed said. "But, I read up on dyslexia yesterday and the day before. Joseph has all the signs. He's an otherwise intelligent child, but for some reason, his brain doesn't process the written word so well. This will help."

Southeby put his hands on his hips.

"Mr. Lazenby, do I have to remind you that you are only a volunteer tutor. You are *not* a credentialcd teacher, and you are definitely not qualified to make a medical diagnosis. I would suggest that you confine yourself to doing what you're told, and leave other matters to those who are more capable of making an informed judgment."

Ed was beginning to feel the heat in his cheeks again. The man just had a way of getting under his skin.

"Has anyone tested him for dyslexia?"

"No," Southeby said, sniffing. "There was no need. The boy just needs to buckle down and study harder."

Ed stood, and in doing so, had to look down at Southeby, who was an inch shorter than Ed's own five-eleven, and considerably smaller of stature. The principal, a shocked look on his face, took a step back.

"How the heck can you say that? I might not be a teacher or a therapist, but even I recognized the signs. He's good at math, and his hand-eye coordination and problem-solving skills are better than many adults. He just doesn't recognize or remember words. I don't need a degree to know what the problem is. Now, why haven't you had him tested?"

"His parents have never expressed a desire for him to be tested, so I saw no reason to do so."

Ed made a growling sound deep in his throat. "What you mean is, if they don't know enough to ask for a service, you'd rather not spend the money on it. That's pretty dam-. Darn bureaucratic, Mister Southeby."

"Now, see here, Lazenby, you can't speak to me in that manner. If you can't follow the rules I set down, your volunteer services can be terminated."

One part of him would've liked nothing better, but Ed felt that no one else was interested in helping

Joseph Garcia, and he'd been drawn to the boy. If he let this officious ass goad him into quitting, he'd be letting Joseph down. He'd learned working at the Pentagon that sometimes, when dealing with bureaucrats, it was better to retreat to fight another day.

"You're right," he said. "I guess I just got a bit overexcited. I assure you, there will be no more frivolity in the sessions."

Southeby sniffed again. "See that there's not." He turned on his heels and strode from the room.

When the door had closed behind him, Ed turned to Joseph and winked. "Don't you worry, kid, these won't be boring sessions. We'll keep doing this, only no more laughing—if we can help it." He turned and stared at the door. "Man, I'd so love to put that turkey's lights out."

As he sat and resumed showing cards to Joseph, he failed to notice the shocked look on Bradley's face.

Charles Ray

CHAPTER 3

After Sotheby left, the rest of Ed's session with Joseph went so well, the encounter with the surly principal ceased to bother Ed. After he went home, though, it all came back. And, when it came back, it made him furious.

He was incensed that the man would have such a stand-offish, bureaucratic attitude when a child's future was at stake, and was, thus, even more determined to do something about it. It bothered him so much that, his scheduled afternoon round of golf with Ernesto was worse than usual, with Ernesto winning every hole by a comfortable stroke margin. Happy at winning so handily, Ernesto hadn't asked him if anything was wrong, and Ed hadn't felt like sharing his feelings.

With little else to do on Thursday, Ed decided to upgrade the cue cards he used with Joseph, reasoning that with better pictures, it would be easier for the boy to make the connection between word and picture. He begged off morning golf, asking Ernesto to reschedule for the afternoon, and around 9:30, hopped into his Toyota 4-Runner and drove to the Office Depot on Shady Grove Road, just west of Route 355. The cavernous store was almost empty of customers when he arrived, and it took him some time browsing the school supply section before he found what he was looking for, a thick stack of heavy cardboard cards with professionally-drawn pictures, underneath which the word describing the picture was printed in bold, black letters. There were fifty cards in the stack, with a wide selection of words, from AARDVARK to ZEBRA, and at $8.50, was a bargain. He looked forward to presenting them to Joseph during their Friday session, which, fortunately was scheduled to start at 9:45, which meant there was little chance that Sotheby could shunt him off to some other meaningless, and irritating duty. Another session with the students in the art class just might make him reconsider continuing his volunteer work.

Friday morning, after having breakfast in the community center dining room with Ernesto and the Wertheim sisters, he let Ernesto talk him into car-pooling, which meant he'd have to hoist himself up into the passenger seat of Ernesto's Ford F-150 pickup, and spend the fifteen-minute ride to Vernon Heights holding onto the dash with a death grip as Ernesto navigated the morning traffic as if he was driving in a demolition derby.

Ernesto chuckled after he'd pulled the Ford into one of the visitor slots in the school parking lot, as luck would have it, right next to the rusty Toyota pickup that Ed knew belonged to the janitor, Thomas

Hadley. He idly wondered why the janitor parked in a visitor slot rather than one of the employee spaces, until he noticed that the maintenance shed, where Hadley kept his tools and supplies, was located adjacent to that part of the parking lot, on the opposite side of the school from the playground. Made sense, he thought, to keep the tools, some of which were sharp and could be dangerous in the hands of unruly, undisciplined, curious teens, as far from where the kids congregated as possible, and it made sense that Hadley would park as close to the shed as possible. The door to the shed, he noticed, was ajar, and a wheelbarrow, containing a variety of gardening tools, sat against the side of the structure. He made a mental note to tell Hadley, when he saw him, that he really shouldn't leave his tools out in the open like that, especially tools like the hoe or shovel, with their sharp edges, which could be dangerous in the hands of a curious child.

He and Ernesto made the hike to the school entrance and entered the hallway, which, because classes were in session, was empty. Their footfalls echoed off the corridor walls as they made their way toward the back of the building, Ernesto to go to the room where he'd been assigned to work with two students on improving their math skills, and Ed to the converted supply room adjacent to the library, where he was anxious to present the new cards to Joseph. At his assigned room, Ernesto stopped.

"We still on for golf this afternoon?" he asked.

"Sure, and don't think I won't pay you back for the last round. I was a bit distracted, or I'd have taken you on the back nine."

Ernesto laughed. "You wish. Okay, into the salt mines. See you at 11:30."

After Ernesto had disappeared behind the closed door, Ed looked at his watch, and noticed that he still had fifteen minutes before his session with Joseph was due to start.

"Maybe I should have a word with Sotheby," he murmured to himself, and then quickly looked around to see if anyone might be nearby who might be a bit taken aback at seeing an elderly gentleman walking the halls talking to himself. The hallway was empty. He breathed a sigh of relief. That would really go over well. If some student had overheard him and reported it to a teacher, or worse, to the principal, he'd never hear the end of it.

He turned and headed back the way he'd come. Sotheby's office was on the opposite side of the school from the library, and just about as far away from the first-floor classrooms as possible. He was pretty sure that Sotheby, if he'd been able, would've had his office in a completely separate building.

The principal's office at Vernon Heights was at the end of a long hallway, the walls of which were covered with photos of sports teams, academic competitions, and other school activities, with Southeby, a sneering smile on his face, prominently featured in each. Where the floors in the rest of the building were either tile or scuffed wood, the floors of this hallway were covered in a cushiony green carpet, and unlike the rest of the school, the walls had a fresh coat of cream-colored paint. During the orientation for the volunteer tutors, Sotheby had complained that the school's lack of adequate funding from the city had necessitated relying on volunteer tutors rather than being able to set up official tutoring programs, but it was obvious from the appearance of the outer regions of his own office that sufficient funds were available to allow him to reign over his dominion in style.

The door to the outer office was closed, which didn't surprise Ed. He remembered from his own days in junior high and high school that the principal's office was forbidden and forbidding territory into which students seldom ventured unless summoned, and when they were summoned, it was rarely for good reasons. Some of the trepidation he remembered experiencing during his own treks to 'see the principal,' came back to him as he approached the door. *Hell fire, I've got nothing to be worried about. I'm not a student, and since I'm not on the payroll, they can't really fire me.*

Taking a deep breath, and squaring his shoulders, he pushed the door open and entered.

The outer office, where Sotheby's personal assistant, as he insisted on calling Augusta Peabody, a slender woman with a slightly hooked nose and piercing green eyes, who had, upon the two occasions Ed had seen her, an expression that was even more sour than Sotheby's, had her office. She was the main gatekeeper, and no one saw the principal without passing by her. But, on this day, the gatekeeper wasn't keeping the gate. The chair behind her desk was empty. A yellow Post-It note attached to one side of the name plate centered precisely on the front edge of her large mahogany wood desk, had OUT RUNNING ERRANDS – BACK IN ONE HOUR printed on it in her obsessively-precise writing. The door to Sotheby's private office, to the left and behind Peabody's desk, was slightly ajar, and Ed could hear the sound of classical music coming from inside.

As he approached the door, an odor, strange, but yet, somehow familiar, hit his nostrils. There was a musky, sceptic-tank smell, the acidic smell of urine, and a coppery odor, all mixed together—altogether unpleasant, and not what he would've expected in the staid confines of Sotheby's inner domain. The closer he drew to the door, the stronger the odor became, and neurons in his brain began cataloging what he was smelling, so that, just before he pushed the door open and stepped into the office, he *knew* what he'd see.

Knowing, and being prepared for it, though, were two entirely different things. He'd been in combat a few times during his years in the army, and had seen death up close and personal more times than he cared to remember. And, he'd never gotten used to it.

He had to clamp his teeth together and swallow hard to keep from throwing up all over the deep, purple carpet. He stopped just inside the door, his muscles locked, unable to move forward or backwards, his eyes taking in the macabre tableau in front of him.

Douglas Sotheby sat in his big leather executive chair, his head back, and his arms splayed to the side. The arrogant sneer that he normally wore had been replaced by a grimace of pain and horror, and his eyes were wide and staring—but seeing nothing. The front of his pearl-colored shirt was covered by a blackish-red shape that looked like one of the art projects from a finger painting class, and in the center of this abstract, amoeba-like shape, the handles of pruning shears stuck out at an upward angle. The shiny black blades of the shears were together, and had been plunged up to half their length into the center of Sotheby's chest. Dark spots on the top of the overly large executive desk showed where arterial spurts had sent blood when the shears were shoved into his chest.

Ed didn't need to get any closer to know that the man was dead, but he finally willed his feet to obey, and he walked closer until he was an inch or two from the front of the desk. From there, the smell of voided bowels and bladder, mixed with the metallic scent of blood, was almost overpowering.

He fought down a momentary sense of panic, forcing his analytical mind to take over. Mentally, he listed the things he should and should not do. One, don't go any closer, and don't touch anything, so as not to contaminate the crime scene. Two, look around and see if he could see any clues as to what had happened—beyond someone shoving pruning shears into the obnoxious principal's chest. And, three, call the police. Actually, he thought, that should've been number two.

He was reaching into his pocket for his phone, when a shriek caused him to freeze in place for half a second, and then to whirl around.

Augusta Peabody, her face paler than usual, and her sneer replaced by a look of horror, and Helen Wheeler, one of the upper grade teachers, also looking horrified, with her mouth wide open, it was clear that she'd been the one who screamed, stood jammed together in the doorway, their eyes moving rapidly from the corpse behind Sotheby's desk to Ed.

"Y-you killed him, you k-killed Mr. Southeby," Wheeler said.

For a second, Ed was paralyzed, Wheeler's words barely penetrating his consciousness. As the two women started moving further into the office, though, he snapped back to awareness, and held up a hand, traffic-cop style, to stop them.

"Whoa, there, don't come in here. This is a crime scene." Suddenly, his mind was clear, and he was thinking analytically again. "And, for your information, I didn't kill him. He was dead when I arrived." He turned halfway and stepped aside to allow them a full view of the corpse. "You see all that blood, and the splatter on the desk? Now, look at me. Do you see any blood on me? No, you don't. If I'd stabbed him, I'd be drenched in blood.

He stepped toward them, causing them to back out and into the secretary's anteroom.

"Now, I'm gonna call 911 and get the police here. You two sit down over there and get yourselves together, so you can answer their questions when they arrive."

Wheeler still looked to be in shock and on the verge of completely losing it. Peabody, on the other hand, after the initial shock, seemed to be thinking clearly. She had, for instance, peered closely at Ed's shirt and hands when he was describing how he'd be covered in blood if he was the killer, and seemed to be nodding in agreement with him.

As he pulled out his phone and dialed, he thought, *This is gonna be one tough day.*

CHAPTER 4

Ed wasn't surprised that despite telling the 911 operator that there was a dead body, and in a middle school of all places, it was over fifteen minutes before he heard the sirens announcing the arrival of the police. The school, unfortunately, happened to be near a neighborhood that was in the transition area between the county's suburban and semi-rural areas, and was located closer to the police station in the adjacent district than that in its own. PVC was in a similar situation, which sometimes resulted in delays in the arrival of the police on those rare occasions when they had a problem.

He went to the door and looked down the hallway. Students and teachers were crowding into the front entrance watching the chaotic scene. He could see heads bobbing and arms waving, teachers and students, as they tried to make sense of what they were seeing. The blue and white flashes from the light bars on the police cruisers flashed through the large glass doors like the glittering disco balls of a bygone era.

Moments later, several uniformed police, their hands on weapons and stern looks on their faces, appeared among the crowd of students and teachers. The lead policeman approached a teacher and leaned toward her. She pointed down the hall toward where Ed was standing with his hands in plain sight. All the policemen headed in his direction, with two men in suits among them. The two men in suits pushed their way to the front and approached Ed.

"Where's the deceased?" the one in front asked, holding up a leather wallet containing a gold detective's shield. "You the one who called this in?"

Ed was careful to keep his voice even and his hands clearly visible. "Yes, officer, I'm Ed Lazenby, a volunteer tutor here. The body, Principal Douglas Southeby, is inside his office."

"I'm *Detective Sergeant* Aubrey Jefferson," the man said, stuffing his badge back into his jacket pocket, which took an effort, because of his portliness and the fact that he hadn't unbuttoned it. He ran a hand through his thinning brown hair, and inclined his head toward the thinner, taller, dark-skinned man to his left, who did have his jacket unbuttoned, and his right hand on the butt of the automatic pistol at his left waist. "This is my partner, Detective Sergeant Sheldon Wayne."

Wayne, whose dark brown head was cleanly shaven and glistening under the ceiling lights, stared at Ed through narrow slits, as if sizing him up. He said nothing; merely nodded.

"Now, Mr. Lazenby, you wanna show us the body?"

Ed stepped aside to let the two detectives enter the secretary's office. One of the armed cops followed them. He pointed to the slightly open door into Sotheby's private office. "It's just through there," he said.

As they entered, they saw Peabody and Wheeler sitting at Peabody's desk.

"And, who is this?" Wayne asked, pointing at them.

The two women shrank into their chairs.

"The one behind the desk is Augusta Peabody. She's, or was, Mr. Sotheby's secretary," Ed said. "The other one is Helen Wheeler, a teacher."

Wayne nodded and made a low snorting sound through his broad nose. "Okay, ladies, we'll want to talk to you later, so hang tight."

Peabody and Wheeler merely nodded in reply, looking blankly at him.

The two detectives approached the door to Sotheby's office.

"Stay close behind us, Mr. Lazenby," Jefferson said. "And, don't touch anything."

Once they were inside the office, Wayne stepped behind Ed and closed the door. The three of them stood there, Ed flanked by the two detectives, and scanned from side to side, finally their gazes coming to rest on the corpse.

"This how you found him?" Jefferson asked.

"Yes," Ed replied.

"Did you touch anything?" Wayne asked from his left side.

Without turning his head to look at the detective, Ed said, "Other than the door when I pushed it open, no, I touched nothing."

He'd recognized that they were about to play interrogation ping pong with him, with each alternating asking questions, probably in an effort to see if they could trip him up. He'd had a friend in the army's Criminal Investigation Division who told him about the technique, one that CID used often to throw an interviewee off balance, and sometimes trick them into saying something implicating. He had nothing to worry about, he reasoned, since he had nothing to hide, but inwardly he resented being treated like a . . . suspect. *Of course! They think that, since I'm the one who found the body, I'm naturally the prime suspect, or at least, that's the way it always is on TV.*

"Why were you here?" Jefferson asked.

"I wanted to talk to him about a young student I'm tutoring." He let it rest there. The other thing he remembered his CID friend telling him was that providing too much information was often a sign of a person trying to mask their guilt. He wasn't guilty of anything, but he also wasn't in any mood to get caught up in their games.

"You know anybody who might want to kill him?" Wayne asked.

"I didn't know him all that well, really. I've only been volunteering here since Monday, and I only met him face to face twice; once at the orientation, and on Wednesday when he came to the room where I'm tutoring."

Wayne walked to the desk and stood there studying the scene carefully. He then turned and looked Ed over, from the top of his head to his shoes, his eyes narrowed in concentration. Finally, he nodded.

"Okay, I think that's all—wait, you're the one who called this in, right?"

"Yes, right after I found him."

Jefferson, apparently the 'good cop' of the duo, stepped up beside his partner, and turned to face Ed.

"Okay then, Mr. Lazenby, you can go," he said. "We might have a few more questions for you, so give your contact information to the officer outside with the two ladies." He then turned to his partner. "I'll let the lab boys in to do their thing before the ME hauls the body away. Why don't you go and talk to the two women, and I'll join you in a few minutes. We'll need to talk to all the staff."

Wayne nodded, and walked to the door. He opened it and stood, his head inclined in Ed's direction. No words were needed for Ed to know that he was being dismissed.

As he past Wayne, the detective said in a low voice, "Don't plan on taking any out of town trips, Mr. Lazenby. I'm pretty sure we're gonna have more questions for you."

Ed was tempted to fire a snappy comeback, but decided against it. For some reason, the black detective seemed to have taken a dislike to him, and he didn't want to fan those flames if he could avoid it.

Back in the anteroom, Wayne seemed to have dismissed Ed from his mind. He turned his attention to Peabody and Wheeler who didn't seem to have moved from their original positions. "I need to talk to each of you," he said. "Is there someplace we can talk privately. The lab techs will be here soon, and this office, in addition to being a restricted crime scene, will be a beehive of activity."

Peabody seemed to snap out of a trance. "A crime scene? Does that mean I won't be able to work at my desk today?"

"I'm afraid so, ma'am. In fact, depending on what the lab boys find, this office might be closed off a couple of days."

"May I take some personal items from my desk?"

He regarded her with his head cocked to one side.

"I suppose so, but I'll have to examine anything you take, you understand."

She frowned, and shot a look at Ed that gave him chills. He looked at his watch. It was already 10:00. He'd missed most of his session with Joseph. But, he could at least present him with the new cards, which were still crammed into his back pocket.

"Detective," he said. "I'm late for my tutoring session, so if you don't need anything else from me, I'll be going."

"Sure, go ahead," Wayne said. "But, give me your contact information first."

After the detective pulled a note book from his jacket, Ed gave him his address and phone number. The way he stared at him as he wrote, made Ed feel uncomfortable.

When Wayne finally snapped his notebook shut and turned back to the two women, Ed slipped out of the office, and made his way through a crowd of policemen and a group of youngish-looking people, three men and one woman, who were heading his way. They paid him no attention as he stepped aside to let them pass. After they'd gone into the office, he turned and continued his journey to the library, hoping that his young charge wasn't too upset at being stood up.

CHAPTER 5

Joseph *had* been concerned at first, but his instructions were to wait for his tutor, and then go to his last class before lunch, so he'd waited. That was another thing Ed really liked about him, unlike other kids his age, he followed instructions. He brightened up when Ed presented him with the new cards, but was curious about all the commotion, so several minutes were wasted as Ed gave him a censored version of events. Other than a slight wrinkling of his brow, and a sad look in his eyes, he hadn't seemed too affected by the news that the principal was dead. Actually, as Ed looked at him, he realized that, other than the shock of finding a dead body, he didn't feel too much about it either. Oh, he wasn't happy that the man was dead, but neither did he feel any great sadness. What he felt was curious. Why did someone so hate the insufferable bureaucrat that he—or, he reminded himself, she—would go to the trouble of shoving something as crude as pruning shears into his chest? And, why take the chance of being seen by doing it in his office during a school day.

It turned out that Joseph was as curious as he was, but curious in the way that only teenage boys can be.

"You really got to see the body, Mr. Ed? Wow, I never saw a dead body before. Was it gross? I bet it was really gross. Was there a lot of blood?"

"Well, it wasn't pleasant, that's for sure. Death never is, and violent death's the worst. Believe me, young man, it's not something you really want to see."

Most people, and not just teens, thought they did, which is why so many people slow down at the scene of accidents, hoping to get a glimpse of the gory bodies. But, the reality was a whole other matter. The sight of a bloody, mangled body could haunt your dreams for years—Ed still remembered some of the ones he'd seen in Vietnam. People think that post-traumatic stress only happens to people who are directly involved in scary events, but that's far from the truth. Witnesses to tragedies can also suffer, sometimes more than the people to whom the tragedies are happening.

For that reason, he felt it unwise to even discuss the case with Joseph. There was no telling what detail might impress itself upon his young mind and lead to future trauma. At the same time, he also knew that it did no good to try and shield young people totally from the uglier side of life, especially those who lived in the local working-class neighborhoods where violence was commonplace.

Joseph, however, was, like all boys his age, curious and persistent.

"Have you seen a lot of dead people?"

"A few." A few too many, Ed thought.

"Were you in the war?" Ed looked at him

quizzically. When asked about his participation in a war, he always thought Vietnam, but he doubted that Joseph even knew the name.

"What war, Joseph?"

"You know, the one over there in Iraq." He pronounced it Eye-rack.

"No, I was in the war in Vietnam, but that was a long time ago."

"But, did you see any people killed in the war?"

Ed shook his head. There was nothing more persistent than a precocious child.

"Yes, in the war, and a few accidents," Ed said. "And, none of them were pleasant. In fact, it upsets me to even think about them." Which was a fact. The conversation was making him decidedly uncomfortable.

"Okay," Joseph said. "I'm sorry, I didn't mean to upset you. Let's play with the cards. Do you have one with a mango on it? I like mangos, and I'd like to know what the word looks like."

Just like that, the boy's mind had switched to another topic. Ed breathed a sigh of relief. He flipped through the cards, looking for the card for words beginning with the letter M.

"Sorry, Joseph, no mangos." He held up the card, which showed a drawing of a restaurant menu, with the word MENU beneath it. "This is close though. Do you know what this is?"

Joseph peered at the card that Ed held up. "Sure, that's a menu. I see them at the Vietnamese restaurant near our house whenever my papa takes us out to eat Vietnamese noodle soup. Do you know what they call their soup?"

Ed laughed.

"I certainly do," he said. "They call it 'phuh,' but they spell it P-H-O. That's because that 'O' in the Vietnamese language is pronounced like the 'u' in the word fur. In fact, the word is like the word 'fur' but without the 'r' sound."

"Wow, you sure know a lot, Mr. Ed."

"Oh, I know that one because I was in Vietnam for a whole year, and while I was there I tried to learn as much of the language as I could."

"Do you know any Spanish?"

Ed had taken Spanish in high school, barely passing the class because at the time his mind was occupied with thoughts of Charlotte Reed, the most beautiful girl in his school, who he'd had a crush on since fourth grade. She sat two desks in front of him in Spanish class, and for most of the period, his eyes were glued to the ponytail that draped over her right shoulder.

"Uh, I think I know a little," he said. "*Mi nombre es Ed.*"

Joseph clapped his hands. "My name is Ed. That's pretty good, Mr. Ed, but that's the way they say it in Spain. In Mexico and Central America, they say *me llamo es Ed.*"

"Really? I didn't know there were different versions of Spanish."

"Oh, yeah. People in El Salvador use different words than those in Mexico, and in Colombia, they sound different than they do in Cuba, and all of them are different from Spain. It's kind of like here in the states, you know, how people from New York sound different than the people from Georgia."

"You're right. I never thought of it that way," Ed said. "You're one smart cookie, Joseph Garcia."

Joseph's smile turned into a frown. "If only I could read. The kids in my class call me the dummy."

"You're not a dummy, you just have trouble recognizing written words. It's called dyslexia, and a lot of people, even adults, have it. But, don't you worry; with these cards, we're gonna teach you to recognize a lot of words."

"So, I won't get held back and have to go to class with the kids who're all younger than me?"

"Exactly. By the time we're done here, you'll ace that reading test. We'll show 'em all."

Just as quickly as the frown had appeared, it disappeared, replaced by a beaming smile. *If only adults were as flexible and adaptable.* Ed began flipping the cards, slowly at first, but as Joseph quickly picked up on the visual cues provided by the drawings, he picked up the pace. He began to believe what he'd told the boy. He *could* teach him to read.

A quick glance at his watch told him that their session was almost up. He began stacking the cards neatly to present them to Joseph. Just as he was passing them across the table, he heard the squeak of the door hinges, announcing someone's arrival. For a fraction of a second, he thought it would be Sotheby, coming to harass him again, until he remembered that the principal wouldn't be harassing him, or anyone else, ever again.

He turned slowly to see who it was, and there, standing in the doorway with a glum look on his dark face, was Detective Wayne. When the man saw him looking, he crooked a finger at him.

"Okay, Joseph, we're done for today. You take these home and practice tonight, and the next time, we'll test you to see how much you remember."

Joseph scooped up the cards and stuffed them into his backpack with the rest of his books. "Okay, Mr. Ed. Thanks for everything. See you next time." He slung the backpack over his shoulders and skipped out, smiling up at the detective as he left.

Wayne stepped into the room and closed the door. His glum look had turned into a scowl.

"We need to talk, Lazenby," he said.

Ed bristled at the form of address and the abrupt tone, but kept his anger in check.

"What about, detective? I told you everything I know already."

"Not everything."

"What could I possible have left out?"

"You conveniently neglected to tell me that earlier this week you threatened to 'put his lights out,' referring, or course, to the recently deceased. And, I believe you called him a turkey."

Ed's mouth flopped open, He was about to object, when he remembered that he had said that very thing—even calling Sotheby a turkey—but, who other than Joseph had heard it? Oh, yes, the janitor was stacking supplies at the time. Must've been him.

"Oh my, that's right, detective," he said. "I'd completely forgotten that. If you have a few minutes, though, I'll explain it fully, and maybe you'll understand why I'd forgotten about it."

Wayne took out his notebook and pen. "I'm all ears," he said.

CHAPTER 6

Ed went over the details of his encounter with Sotheby, culminating in his unfortunate statement. As he spoke, Wayne scribbled furiously in his notebook. When he was done, he snapped the book shut, and without saying whether or not he believed Ed's version of events, reminded him not to leave town, and left him standing alone in the room, completely bewildered.

During the ride back to PVC, he stared vacantly out the window of Ernesto's pickup, answering in monosyllables whenever Ernesto asked him a question, but otherwise silent.

When they arrived at PVC, Ernesto pulled the pickup into Ed's driveway and shut off the engine.

"Okay, Ed," he said. "Something's bugging you, and I ain't leavin' until you spill."

Ed heaved a sigh. "Okay, let's go inside, and I'll make a pot of coffee. I think coffee and a nip or two of whiskey is required if I'm to make sense of what happened today."

Ernesto was mercifully silent while Ed put coffee on to brew, and even waited without a word as the coffee bubbled in the pot. Finally, when they were seated in Ed's living room, a pot of steaming coffee, a bottle of Jim Beam, two tumblers and two white ceramic mugs on the coffee table in front of them, he broke the silence.

"Okay now, amigo," he said. "What the hell's got your panties in a twist?"

"You know I was the one that found Sotheby's body this morning, right?"

"Yeah, I heard a couple of the teachers sayin' it was you, his secretary, and that cute teacher, Helen Wheeler."

"Actually, *I* found the body. I went to his office to see if I could get him to test this kid I'm tutoring for dyslexia, and found him there with a pair of pruning shears stuck in his chest. The ladies came in afterwards."

Ernesto took a sip of whiskey, a sip of coffee, and then another sip of whiskey. He smacked his lips. "Okay, so you found the body. I guess that'd upset me too, a little. But, I got me this feelin' that there's more to it."

"There is." Ed picked up the coffee mug, put it down and picked up the tumbler half full of whiskey. He took a long swallow. "You see, earlier this week, I had a bit of a run-in with Sotheby, and I might've said something about wanting to hurt him. Unfortunately, somebody overheard me and told the cops."

Ernesto shrugged. "I only met the guy once, when we went through orientation, but from that one time, I imagine just about everybody in the school didn't like him. How's that upsetting you?"

"Because, I think the police, at least that Detective

Wayne, think I might've killed him."

Ernesto paused, the glass of whiskey halfway to his mouth, and stared goggle-eyed at Ed.

"You're kidding, right?"

"I wish I was," Ed said. He took another sip of whiskey, set the glass down and picked up the mug of coffee, holding it under his nose and breathing in the aroma. "I could tell the moment he first saw me that he suspected me. Makes sense, I suppose. After all, I found the body, and the first person on the scene in often the guilty party. But, the look in his eyes when he confronted me about saying I wanted to put Sotheby's light out left no doubt . . . he thinks that I somehow did it."

"But, you didn't . . . right?"

Ed's brows rose half an inch. "Not you, too!"

"Naw, just bustin' your chops, man. I know you wouldn't do nothin' like that, and I can't believe the cops seriously think you did. 'Sides, if you stabbed someone in the chest wouldn't you be all covered with blood or something?"

Ed nodded vigorously. "Damn right you would. I mean, there was blood spatter all the way to the front edge of the desk."

"Well, there you have it. You're still wearin' the same clothes you had on this morning, and I don't see any blood."

"I think that's the only reason Wayne hasn't arrested me."

Ernesto put a finger on the side of his nose. "Now, I understand why he was asking me the questions he did," he said.

"Questions, what questions?"

"Well, they talked to all the teachers, along with me and Rose and Violet, you know, askin' if we'd seen anything. He asked if I'd seen you, and I told him you and me rode in together. Then, he asked if you and Sotheby got along. I told him I didn't think you even knew him all that well, but that you got along with just about everybody."

"Thanks for that. If he asks again, be sure and tell him about the clothes, okay?"

"You think he might?"

Ed laughed. "Hell, man, I don't know. I got a feeling they didn't have a clue who did it, and he was just grabbing at straws."

"Hey, what about his secretary? She'd be able to tell 'em you didn't do it, wouldn't she?"

"Nah." Ed shook his head. "She was out of her office when I arrived, running an errand or something."

"So, what're we gonna do?"

What, indeed? Ed felt between a rock and a hard place. He was pretty sure that if the police *really* believed that he'd killed Sotheby, he'd already be behind bars. But, he also knew that as the case drug on, if they didn't find another suspect, in their desire to close the case, they just *might* focus on him, and even though he knew he was innocent, that would be uncomfortable. The only way he could think to keep that from happening was to find out who *did* kill Sotheby.

"We're gonna solve this case, is what we're gonna do," he said.

CHAPTER 7

The first step of Ed's solution was to call Carl Janzen. A senior detective with the Montgomery County Police Ed had met when Violet, staging a fake kidnapping had been actually kidnapped, Janzen had become a friend of sorts over the time Ed had known him, albeit a somewhat grudging friendship because of Ed and Ernesto's annoying habit of sticking their noses into police investigations. That they'd helped solve a couple of tough cases only slightly moderated Janzen's objections to civilians dabbling in police matters. Shortly after his first visit to PVC, one that resulted in the arrest of the kidnappers of Violet Wertheim, one of whom was the boyfriend of PVC's dietician and dining room manager, Janet Murphy, Janzen and Murphy had become an 'item,' causing him to spend much of his free time there. This, actually, was what had finally pushed his relationship with Ed into the friendship category. Ed took a chance, and invited the detective for a late lunch, not surprised when Janzen immediately agreed, motivated more by his desire, Ed was certain, to see Janet than to sample PVC's culinary delights, or enjoy Ed's company.

He caught Janzen just about to leave his office for lunch, and when he invited him to join him and Ernesto for lunch at PVC, the detective said he'd be there in half an hour. This gave them just enough time to wash their faces and get to the dining facility before he arrived. Ed's plan was to get there, and talk Janet into joining them for lunch. That proved to be surprisingly easy.

"Of course, I'll join the three of you," she said after Ed asked if she minded eating with Ernesto, Carl Janzen, and him. "And, we're not doing buffet. You let me plan the menu, and I'll get it brought to the table." When Ernesto looked uncertain, she said, "Don't worry. I know what you like, and I guarantee you'll like what I select. Now, go grab a table. Carl will be here any minute now."

They headed for Ed's usual table in the corner near a window, with a view of the entrance and the rest of the dining room, and somewhat separated from the other tables. He and Ernesto had long ago staked out this particular table as 'theirs,' and except for a few hardheaded people who'd tried once or twice to challenge them for it, it was left vacant.

"Should we have invited Rose and Violet?" Ernesto asked as they grabbed glasses of iced tea from the beverage table and headed to the table.

"No, I'd like to talk to Carl before I share anything with them. You know how Rose worries, and Violet's likely to go off and do something rash. Before we involve them, we need a plan."

He knew that once he and Ernesto started digging into Sotheby's murder, there was no way he could keep Rose and Violet from becoming involved. The four of them were considered something of a crime-solving quartet in PVC, giving them a kind of celebrity status with everyone—everyone except the CEO of PVC, Roland Vickers, who was, in his own way, as much of an annoying, officious bureaucrat as Sotheby had been.

After taking a sip of tea, Ernesto put his glass down and leaned forward with his elbows on the table, something he'd be castigated about by Rose if she were present—the Wertheims, despite being born and bred in suburban Maryland, often put on southern antebellum airs, and Violet, especially, thrived on correcting other people, whether it was their table manners or way of speaking, it didn't matter—she just loved putting people in what she called their 'proper' place.

"I guess you're right," he said. "Heaven knows, once Violet hears that you're a suspect in a murder, she'll never let you hear the last of it unless you got a plan to catch the real killer. I'm curious, though; how is Carl gonna help us? I now he's a friend, sort of, but he's still a cop. You think he's gonna put his neck on the line helpin' a murder suspect?"

"Well, for starters, I'm hoping he'll use his noggin and see that there's no way anyone could seriously believe I killed Sotheby. Then, I'll try to get him to tell us everything he knows about the case."

"Which you know he ain't gonna do."

"Not directly, no," Ed said. "Then again, I didn't plan on asking him directly."

"You gonna use that black box stuff you learned in the Pentagon?"

Ed looked shocked. "I did not learn any black box stuff at DOD, and you well know it. I was just a systems analyst. But, over the years, I have learned how to talk to and listen to people. You'd be surprised what you can learn just by listening."

Ernesto glanced toward the entrance. "Well, you're about to get your chance. Here he comes."

Wearing his trademark rumpled suit, a medium blue one today, Senior Detective Carl Janzen shuffled through the entrance. He knew that Ed and Ernesto had their favorite table, so he didn't even bother looking around for them, just made a sharp left turn as he entered, and made a beeline for the table.

"Hey, guys," he said as he approached the table. Although he had what passed for him as a pleasant expression, Ed noticed that his gaze lingered a bit as their eyes locked. "Thanks for the invite. I would've had to eat at a fast food place otherwise."

"Our pleasure," Ed said. "Janet will be joining us. She's also preparing a special lunch, I'm sure because you're with us."

Janzen's craggy face darkened and he ducked his head. "Uh, well, that's nice." He glanced up at Ed. "She's not cooking it, is she?"

Ed smiled. Apparently, Janet had demonstrated her lack of cooking skills for Janzen. She was a sweet girl, but she couldn't boil water without making a mess. "No," he said. "She has a professional chef who does all the cooking. She only prepares the menu, and that's something she's very good at."

Janzen sat in the chair opposite Ed and smiled. "Don't tell her I said anything, but boy do I wish she knew how to cook. When I take her out, if we don't eat here, we have to go to some restaurant, and it's beginning to eat a hole in my budget."

"I guess we'll just have to invite you to eat with us here more often," Ed said. "I'm sure Janet would like that. It'd give her more chances to see you."

Just then, the subject of their conversation emerged from the door to the kitchen, followed by two of the dining center workers, slender, middle-aged ladies who kept the buffet lines stocked and saw to the needs of the more infirm residents. As they neared, Ed could see that Janet had pulled out all the stops. What they were bringing wasn't just an ordinary lunch, it resembled a holiday meal.

Ernesto's mouth gaped open when the two women began putting the food in the center of the table. There was a ham, a whole ham, roasted a golden brown, a bowl of fluffy white mashed potatoes, a platter of chicken drumsticks, creamed corn, some kind of dark green leafy vegetable, fried yellow squash, a big bowl of tossed salad that had bacon bits sprinkled liberally on it, and a tray of corn muffins. Janet stood there, looking at Janzen with a big smile on her face as the women worked.

"Wow, this is a lot of food," Janzen said. "I was expecting just a simple lunch."

"If you look at the buffet line," Janet said. "You'll see that this is just the simple lunch that everyone else is having. I just took a ham before they sliced it for the counter, and had them put the other things in more festive containers."

"It sure looks different served this way," Ernesto said.

"That it does," Ed said. "Come on, Janet, sit

yourself down and join us. You know Carl came here for you, and not the food."

Janzen's cheeks turned red. "Well, actually, I came for both." He smiled at Janet. "But, I would've come even if there was no food."

She blushed and smiled back at him. "I know." She pulled out the chair next to him and sat. "Now, let's eat."

Bowls and platters were passed around, and everyone helped themselves to generous helpings of everything. They ate for a few minutes in silence, but Janzen kept glancing at Ed as he ate. Finally, he put his fork down and leaned forward, his jacket becoming more wrinkled as he pressed against the table edge.

"Okay, Ed," he said. "I know you have something on your mind. Not that I have any objection to having lunch with you guys, but I think I've known you long enough now to know when something's up, so spill it."

Ed put his utensils down and leaned back in his chair. He looked at Ernesto who nodded and smiled wanly.

Taking a deep breath, he said, "I guess you know about the principal over at Vernon Heights Middle School getting killed?"

Janzen frowned. "Yeah, I heard. Terrible thing, that."

"I don't suppose you can talk about it, it being an active case and all?"

"If it was my case, I couldn't talk about it at all, you know that. But, I'm not the lead investigator on this case, so there's not a helluva lot I know, even if I could tell you."

"Is Detective Wayne the lead?"

"Nah, Sheldon's the junior in that partnership. Aubrey Jefferson's in charge."

"Are they making any progress in finding out who might have done such a terrible thing?"

Janzen steepled his stubby fingers and rested his chin on them. He had a sad expression on his crabby face.

"Look Ed," he said. "I shouldn't be telling you this. If it ever got out, I could get suspended. But, they, well, Wayne at least, have their eyes on a suspect. Problem is they don't have a solid motive, and bupkis as far as hard evidence is concerned."

Ed leaned forward. "It's me he suspects, right?"

Janet gasped audibly. "You? Ed, how could anyone think you would kill someone?"

Janzen's eyes widened, but Ed thought he was feigning surprise for Janet's benefit, because she was looking at him with an accusatory stare.

"Carl," she said. "Tell him that's not true. No one suspects Ed Lazenby is a murderer . . . right?"

"That's okay, Carl, you can tell her," Ed said. "I suppose, under the circumstances, I can almost see Detective Wayne's reasoning, despite the fact that there is no evidence."

Janzen smiled weakly. "Like I said, no evidence, so that means there's really no viable suspect."

"Which, unfortunately, because of my ill-advised comment about the victim, leaves me directly in Wayne's crosshairs."

"So, Ed, you admit to saying you wanted to put Sotheby's lights out?"

"Well, sure I said it, but it was in the heat of the moment, and was justified by the circumstances." He proceeded to explain them, ending with that being the reason he was in Sotheby's office, and had been the one to discover the body. "You see, he was ignoring this student's true condition, and planning to hold him back a grade, and I felt, feel, that's the wrong way to go. I was going to try and argue my case for an examination once again. But, I never got the chance." Ed shrugged.

"Well, for what it's worth," Janzen said. "I don't think you did it. If nothing else, there would've been at least a bit of blood splatter on you, and even Wayne admits that there was none. But, also, I know you, and I know you're no murderer. All the same, though, I think it might be a good idea for you to consult a lawyer . . . just in case Wayne gets a bug up his ass."

Ed laid a finger against his nose, and stared down at his plate. Finally, he slapped the table and looked across at Janzen. "You know, I considered that, but I've decided against it, for now at least. I know having legal advice is wise, but if I hired a lawyer right now, before even being formally accused, it would look like I *might* have something to hide. No, I need to deal with this in another way."

"No, don't tell me you're planning to try and find the killer yourself." Janzen was shaking his head.

"It's one sure way to prove it wasn't me, don't you think?"

Still shaking his head, Janzen said, "It's also a good way to get yourself arrested for interfering in a police investigation."

"I don't plan on interfering," Ed said. "Just doing a little snooping around the edges to make sure nothing important gets missed."

"Ed, please. I know I've been lax in the past with you guys sticking your noses in police business, but—"

"Haven't we produced results?"

"Well, yeah, but this time's different. If they consider you a suspect, anything you do could be seen as trying to cover your tracks, or divert the investigation. You could get yourself into a lot of trouble."

"In that case, I guess we'll just have to be extra careful, won't we?"

"Good grief," Janzen said. "You guys will be the death of me yet."

Charles Ray

CHAPTER 8

Disgruntled and out of sorts as he was at Ed's announcement that he'd be investigating the murder, Janzen still managed to polish off all the food on his plate *and* flirt with Janet at the same time, much to Ernesto's amusement. Finally, resigned to the fact that he wouldn't be able to convince Ed and his friends to stay on the sidelines, he cautioned him to be careful, kissed Janet on the cheek—causing her to blush deeply—and left.

Ed reassured a worried Janet that he hadn't killed anyone, and that nothing bad was going to happen, and then he and Ernesto walked back to his place to work out a plan of investigation.

Just as they were approaching Ed's front door, he heard Violet's strident voice from behind.

"Hey, you two," she said. "Why didn't you invite us to join you for lunch?"

Ed paused, his hand on the door knob, and looked over his shoulder. He shot Ernesto a warning look. "Uh, I had some private stuff to discuss with Carl Janzen," he said.

"You mean about you being a murder suspect?" Violet's tone was accusatory.

"How—"

"Janet called us as soon as you left the dining room," Rose said. Her voice had a worried tenor. "Is it true?"

Ed could only shrug. He should've known that Janet Murphy wouldn't be able to keep such news to herself, and that she'd naturally tell his only other friends about his 'trouble.'

"Why don't you guys come inside," he said. "We can talk about it. Who's up for coffee?"

"I'd prefer tea," Rose said.

"I think something stronger is called for," said Violet.

"For once, I find myself agreeing with Violet," Ernesto chimed in.

"I suppose I do, too," Ed said. "Okay, I'll brew coffee *and* tea, and we still have nearly three-quarters of that bottle of Jim Beam we were working on "

With his three guests seated in the living room, and Ernesto pouring himself a generous helping of Jim Beam, Ed went into the kitchen and brewed fresh pots of coffee and tea. When that was done, he placed the carafes of tea and coffee on a large plastic tray along with four cups, sugar and cream containers, and four spoons. Back in the living room, he put the tray in the center of the coffee table.

"Okay, help yourselves," he said. Then, while they filled their cups with the beverage of their choice, he poured himself half a water glass of whiskey, and took a long sip. "Ah, that feels good."

He placed the glass down and took a chair opposite

Ernesto and looked at the Wertheim sisters who were sitting on the sofa, Violet drinking coffee, and Rose blowing across the rim of the steaming cup of tea she'd poured for herself. After taking two tentative sips of coffee, Violet put her cup on the table and faced Ed, a concerned look on her face.

"Now, Ed Lazenby," she said. "It's time you told us what in Hades is going on."

"You, of course, know about the principal being killed in his office," he said.

Violet waved her hands dismissively. "Of course, we know about that. It was all over the school, not that we needed it, with the police crawling all over the place and asking a thousand questions. You found the body, right?"

"Yes. I went to office to talk to him about having young Joseph Garcia tested for dyslexia, and found him there with a pair of pruning shears in his chest."

"Oh, my goodness," Rose said. "That must have been awful."

Ed shuddered. "It's not exactly how I would've liked my day to start."

"Do the police have any idea who might've done it?" Violet asked.

Ed paused. He knew his next words would not go down well at all. "Well, I can't be absolutely sure, but, I think one of the detectives investigating the case thinks that I might've done it."

At first, there was nothing but silence. Then, Violet and Rose started talking at the same time.

"That's ridiculous!"

"Oh, my. Why on earth would they think you would kill Principal Sotheby? You hardly knew him." Rose, of course, was a bit more sympathetic than her older sister.

'Well, for starters, I was the one who found the body, and the police just usually look at the first person on the scene as a suspect. It's just the way their minds work."

"I repeat, ridiculous," Violet said. "Why on earth would you have any reason to kill a man you only met this week?"

"Uh, well, it seems that someone overheard me saying that I'd like to put his lights out."

Rose almost lost control of her tea cup, only catching it at the last moment, but still spilling some on her skirt.

"W-why would you say such a thing, Ed?"

He explained his confrontation with Sotheby over whether or not Joseph Garcia was learning disabled or, as Sotheby seemed to have thought, just a poor student. "It was just one of those things you say when a bureaucrat has ruffled your feathers. I was mostly talking to myself, although young Joseph was there."

"He told the police what you said?"

"No, Joseph would never do that. Unfortunately, the janitor, Tom Hadley, was also there, but he was working so quietly in the corner, I'd forgotten he was even there. I'm sure, though, that he's the one who told the police what I said."

"So, what do we do now?" Ernesto asked.

"Simple, really, we find out who did kill Sotheby," Ed said. "We make a list of possible suspects, and discretely check them out . . . hopefully, without the police knowing we're doing it."

Ernesto nodded. "Yeah, wouldn't do for the cops to

know their prime suspect's investigatin' the case."

Violet picked up a spoon and rapped the side of her cup. Everyone turned toward her.

"The first suspect on our list has to be Hadley," she said.

"The janitor? Why?' Ernesto asked.

She sent a withering glare his way, causing him to shrink back in his chair. "Well, for starters, he pointed the police your way, and then, there's the weapon," she said, holding up a finger. "Who at that school has the most access to pruning shears?" Without waiting for a reply, she continued, "The janitor, of course. He's also the groundskeeper, isn't he?"

"As a matter of fact," said Ed. "He is. And, he has the key to the tool shed where those shears were supposed to be kept." Then, he remembered that what he'd seen when he and Ernesto arrived that morning. "Of course, this morning, when we arrived, the shed was open, and there were gardening tools outside in the open."

"Did you see pruning shears, either of you?"

"We weren't really close enough to tell if they were there or not," he said.

"So, this Hadley person could've already had them and killed Sotheby with them before you even entered the school building."

Ed snapped his finger. "You're right. I don't recall seeing him anywhere until after the police arrived. Besides, he's the only person who could've been walking around with pruning shears without it looking strange. He probably wouldn't even have been noticed."

"So," Ernesto said. "He had the means, and

probably the opportunity. All we need to do is establish the motive, and we can tell the police. That oughta make them stop thinking you did it."

It sounded good, Ed thought, almost too good, in fact. "Finding out the motive isn't gonna be easy."

"Yeah, how're we gonna do that?"

He thought about it for a few seconds. "I have an idea. We'll do it in two phases—actually two simultaneous steps—you and I will ask around the school to try and determine what his relationship with Sotheby was; Violet, you and Rose need to keep a watch on Hadley. See where he goes, what he does, and who he talks to. Can you do that?"

"We can." Violet said. "But, I think you two guys would be better for the following, and you should let Rose and me do the questioning. People are more likely to talk to women than a man, especially since most of the rest of the staff at Vernon Heights just happens to be female."

"Okay, good point. Fine, then, Ernesto and I will tail Hadley. You start snooping around and see if you can find out whether or not Hadley had any kind of grudge against the principal."

Violet picked up her glass, half full of whiskey, and held it high. "All right! This is more like it. Things were beginning to get boring around here."

Except for Rose, who lifted her tea cup, the others hoisted their whiskey and joined her.

"My friends," Ed said. "As Sherlock Holmes would say, the game's afoot."

CHAPTER 9

Ed and Ernesto started their stakeout of Hadley in earnest the next day, by arriving at Vernon Heights early. They found parking in a strip mall a few blocks south of the school, and walked back, entering the parking lot reserved for visitors from a copse of trees at the corner farthest from Hadley's tool shed at 6:50.

At the edge of the lot, Ed stopped and looked over the lot. "I don't see Hadley's old truck, do you?" he asked Ernesto.

"Naw, me neither. Guess we got here before him. So, how we gonna play this?"

"I'm thinking we should split up," Ed said. "One of us should watch the employee parking lot, just in case he decides to park there for a change. Why don't you go there, and I'll hang out here?"

Ernesto nodded his agreement and trotted off toward the employee parking lot. Ed backed into the copse of trees, found a place where he could see the tool shed and rest his back against the trunk of a good-sized tree, and settled in to wait.

He'd barely gotten himself settled comfortably

against the tree when Hadley's battered old pickup, belching gray smoke, noisily entered the parking lot. As Ed had expected he would, he parked in a space as close to the tool shed as possible and turned off the ignition. Then, to Ed's surprise, he sat there, his arms resting on the steering wheel, and looked around, peering right and left like he was looking for someone, or, Ed thought, looking to see if he was being watched.

As quickly as he'd had the thought, Ed dismissed it. There was no way Hadley could know that Ed and Ernesto would be watching him, no way at all. Nonetheless, he shrank back against the tree trunk and tried to make himself smaller. Not that he thought that Hadley could see him; it would've been impossible to distinguish his body in the deep shadows cast by all the trees surrounding him, but out of an atavistic response to the fact that the man was looking in his direction. He froze in place, hardly daring to breathe, until Hadley's gaze shifted.

Slowly, still glancing from side to side, Hadley made his way to the tool shed. He looked around furtively, before reaching into the pocket of his grimy overalls and extracting a shiny brass key which he inserted into the big padlock in the chain looped through the handles of the shed's double doors. He looked around once more before pulling the doors open and slipping inside the shed, pulling them closed behind him.

Now, that was strange. Why would he be sneaking into his own tool shed? I wonder what's inside there. With that thought, Ed made a decision that he hoped he wouldn't later regret. He remembered something an old sergeant had told him when he was in the army, 'keep your friends close, but your enemies closer.' He wouldn't watch Hadley from hiding, but from up close, up close and personal. Besides, he thought, I have a reason to talk to him; I want to confirm that he's the one who told the police about my indiscrete remark about Sotheby.

The decision made, he left his hiding place in the trees, and walked across the parking lot toward the tool shed.

The doors were pulled tightly closed, but he could hear the sounds of movement from inside the metal-walled shed. He debated just opening the doors, but decided it might not be a good idea to just barge in. He rapped lightly on the wood frame, and waited a few seconds. The sounds of movement stopped. When there was no answer, he rapped again, louder this time. He heard the sound of footsteps approaching the doors.

He had to step back when the doors began swinging open, but they only opened enough to allow Hadley to fill the space between them. He was frowning, and his eyes were bloodshot.

"Yeah? Oh, Mr. Lazenby," he said, blinking. "What can I do for you?" He squinted at Ed and cocked his head to the side. "Say, you're here awful early. You're not supposed to be here until 9:30."

"I came early, Mr. Hadley, because I wanted to talk to you.

"Oh. Whatcha need from me?"

Ed knew that from this point he should tread carefully, but no matter how carefully he tried to phrase it, he was likely to alienate the man. So, he decided to just say it straight out.

"I just wondered if it was you that told the police I

said I'd like to put Mr. Sotheby's lights out?"

Hadley looked away momentarily, something like guilt flickering in his eyes.

"Uh, well, yeah," he said. "I hope it didn't get you into any trouble. It's just, they asked me if I knew anybody who didn't like the principal, or anybody who'd ever said anything negative about him, you know. I heard what you said that day in the room when he was givin' you a hard time about the Garcia boy. I couldn't lie to the police and say I'd never heard nothin'. You can understand that, can't you?"

"Sure, I understand. I just wanted to be sure."

"I mean, I don't think you kilt him or nothin' like that."

Too bad you didn't tell the police that. Or, did you? Maybe that's why they haven't taken me in. Focus, Ed. Keep your mind on the case. "Do you know anyone here who might want to hurt him?"

Hadley chuckled, a gruff sound, accompanied by a dribble of spittle from the corner of his mouth. "You only knew him a little while, but I reckon you can figure out that most people here didn't like him too much. He was always lordin' it over other people, like he was some kind of royalty."

"Do you think he ever offended anyone enough that they might want to kill him?"

"Nah, just mutter about him, kinda like you did."

Ed started to turn away, then he stopped. "By the way, you know he was killed with pruning shears."

"Yeah, they come from my tool shed," Hadley said. His face contorted in a painful expression.

"Really? How do you know that?"

"I know 'cause I got my initials, T.H., carved in the

handle of every tool. When the police showed 'em to me, sure enough, my initials was there, and I noticed just before all the commotion started that my shears was missin' from the shed."

"I noticed that you had a lot of tools outside the shed that morning," Ed said. "Why was that?"

"I was plannin' to trim the bushes near the softball field, so I come in early and put the tools out. I had to go to the boiler room for my work gloves, and while I was there, I noticed the boiler was actin' up, so I took some time to fix it. Then, I come back out, grabbed the wheelbarrow and went to the ball field. It was there I noticed the shears was gone. I know they was there when I went inside. I figured maybe a student had come by and taken 'em, and was just about to go in and talk to Mr. Sotheby when all them police cars started pullin' up."

"So, the tools were out in the open, unguarded, for a while. How long do you reckon?"

"Musta been 'bout thirty, forty-five minutes, mebbe more. I wasn't payin' too much attention to time."

"And, you didn't see anyone around here when you came back out?"

"No, I-, say, you ask an awful lotta questions for a volunteer. You sound almost like a cop. Why you wanta know all this stuff?"

Uh-oh, time for a tactical retreat. "Sorry, I'm just nosy, is all. Ask any of the other volunteers, they'll tell you. I'm sort of an amateur detective; always sticking my nose in anything that looks suspicious."

"Well, there ain't no more I can tell you. Somebody took my prunin' shears and stuck 'em in old man Sotheby's chest. I'm sorry the old coot's dead, but I can tell you, there probably ain't nobody gonna really mourn his passin'. Anyway, I got to get to work. I never did get them bushes pruned. Had to talk Miss Peabody into givin' me petty cash to buy a new pair of prunin' shears, 'cause the police say my old one's evidence in a murder case, so they done confiscated 'em."

Ed began backing away. "Sorry to interfere with your schedule," he said. "I'll let you get back to work now."

Hadley said nothing as Ed turned and began walking toward the school building. As he reached the front of the school, he turned and looked back. Hadley was standing in front of the tool shed, looking from the parking lot, empty except for his pickup, to Ed, and even at that distance, Ed could tell that he had a puzzled expression on his face. He quickly pushed open the entrance door and entered the lobby.

Inside, he paused and caught his breath. He mentally reviewed what he'd learned from Hadley—which wasn't much. He only had the man's word that someone else had taken his shears. He had, by his own admission, been inside the building around the time the murder might've taken place. The weapon used had belonged to him. And, he didn't seem to think too much of the victim. Motive, means, and opportunity. But, Ed still wasn't convinced. While he wasn't yet prepared to rule him out entirely, he was having a hard time seeing the janitor as a murderer. Oh, he was hiding something; of this there seemed no doubt. Ed hadn't failed to notice that he carefully blocked his view inside the tool shed. But, could that be a motive for murder? It would take a lot more snooping around to determine that.

After waiting a few minutes, he went back outside, looking toward the tool shed without being too obvious about it. It proved unnecessary, though, for Hadley was nowhere in sight. He sighed and headed toward the staff parking lot in search of Ernesto.

Charles Ray

CHAPTER 10

After meeting up, Ed and Ernesto walked back to where they'd parked. Still too early for their tutoring sessions, they went to a Starbucks in the area and sat and chatted over large coffees until a few minutes before they were due to report to the school.

For Ed, the morning went by too slowly. Although he enjoyed his session with young Joseph, who was showing great progress after only one day of using the new flash cards, he was anxious to get back to the investigation. Most importantly, he wanted to find out if Violet and Rose had learned anything useful.

When their tutoring sessions were finished, Ed and Ernesto accepted Rose's invitation to join her and Violet for lunch at their place.

Back at the Wertheim residence, they made small talk while Rose and Violet put a lunch of tuna sandwiches, chips, and lemonade together. They sat around the dining table, eating silently at first, but after finishing his chips and half of his sandwich, Ed could restrain his curiosity no longer. He put the half sandwich back on the plate and pushed back from the table.

"Okay, let's talk about what we learned today, folks," he said. "I'll start if you don't mind." He then told them about his conversation with Hadley.

"You actually went up and talked to him," Ernesto said around a mouth full of sandwich. "Was that wise?"

"It seemed the thing to do at the time. I learned a few things from him. I'm not sure they're helpful, but, hey, I got tired of lurking in the trees."

"What if he's the killer? He might think you're on to him, and you could be in danger."

"He's hiding something," Ed said. "But, I don't think he's the killer. I think someone happened along and saw his tools unsecure and took that pair of shears."

"And, just what makes you think it wasn't him?" Violet asked.

"Call it an instinct I have for detecting falsehood. I developed the ability to detect bull crap when I worked in the Pentagon. Believe me, the only place I know that produces more lies than the Pentagon is congress."

"Don't forget the White House," Ernesto said.

"Oh, yeah. That place is in a class all by itself with the current occupant right now." In the previous year's election, he'd voted for the other candidate, and like millions of others, had been shocked when her opponent won the Electoral College despite losing the popular vote by several million. He still couldn't bring himself to utter the man's name. "Anyway, I know Hadley's up to something, but I don't think it has anything to do with the murder. I just don't see his motive."

"Speaking of motive," Rose said. "Why don't you tell

him what we learned to day, Violet?"

All heads turned to look at Violet. She smiled, enjoying being the center of attention.

"Just before we started our tutoring session," she said. "I was talking to two of the other teachers. Well, actually, I was just standing there eavesdropping. Anyway, they were mentioning Sotheby's girlfriend, and how his death must have her devastated."

"Girlfriend? Wasn't he married?" Ed asked.

"Apparently, he wasn't satisfied with just one woman. He'd apparently hit on several of the women teachers. Since it's a violation of school system rules, they turned him down, all except one."

"Well, don't keep us in suspense, who is it?" Ed asked.

Violet let the suspense hang in the air until she could feel the tension vibrating from her audience of three. Just as Ed snarled and opened his mouth to speak, she said, "It's Helen Wheeler. She and the principal were having an affair."

"Holy shit," Ernesto said. "Oops, excuse my French."

Rose smiled. "I'd never talk like that, but I was thinking the same thing."

"That explains why she screamed," Ed said.

Violet looked at him. "Screamed? When?"

"When she and Augusta Peabody walked in after I'd found the body, Helen screamed, and accused me of killing him. I didn't think anything of it at the time, figured it was just the shock of seeing a dead body. But, now, it makes sense."

"Darn," Violet said. "And, here I was thinking she'd make a good suspect."

"Your news gives me another one, though," he said. "Peabody didn't scream. In fact, she didn't show a lot of emotion. She worked closely with Sotheby, and if he was the rogue you paint him out to be, it's a good chance he was also involved with her. Maybe she was jealous that he'd moved on to Wheeler."

"My, my, this just keeps getting better and better." Violet rubbed her hands together. "Vernon Heights is like a Peyton Place. Rose, you and I have some more snooping to do."

Ed nodded. "You certainly do. Find out how long Wheeler and Sotheby were a . . . thing, and see if there are any rumors of anything between him and Peabody. The note on her desk said she was out, but she could've killed him before leaving, and, because she's who she is, she could move around the school freely, and I doubt if anyone would notice her."

"You think she took the janitor's shears and did her boss?" Ernesto asked.

"That, my friend, is what we have to find out."

CHAPTER 11

There was little they could do over the weekend, so Ed and Ernesto played golf on Saturday and Sunday mornings—now that he was doing something constructive, his game had improved—and, after golf, spent both afternoons with Violet and Rose mapping out their activities for the coming week.

Even though he was pretty sure Thomas Hedley was not the murderer they sought, he decided that discretion was the better course to take, so he asked Ernesto to continue keeping an eye on him. Rose and Violet would continue to see what gossip they could pick up from the faculty. His task would be to approach Helen Wheeler and see what he could learn from her. His reason for that, he explained to them, was that he was more likely to pick up on any evasion she might attempt. Violet wasn't convinced of his ability to detect lies, but the prospect of doing more and wider snooping was so tempting, she didn't argue much.

But, as an exchange for agreeing to let Ed talk to Wheeler rather than her, Violet insisted that they all car pool to school in her car, a dark blue, 1980 Chrysler Cordoba, a big boat of a car that got even fewer miles per gallon than Ernesto's pickup. The only advantage it had over the truck was that Ed didn't have to step up to get inside, but, because Rose wanted to sit next to Ernesto, and the two of them took the back seat, he had to sit up front with Violet, and Violet was what he would call an aggressive driver. She made Ernesto's driving seem like a Sunday outing by a doddering senior citizen, the way she weaved in and out of traffic, changed lanes suddenly without signaling, and generally viewed other drivers with disdain.

By the time they arrived at the school parking lot, his knuckles were aching from gripping the dashboard, and his jaw sore from clenching his teeth. He decided not to comment on Violet's driving, but was seriously considering calling a cab to go home when their stint of tutoring was done.

William Chertoff, the physical education teacher and coach of the boys' football and basketball teams, stopped them just as they entered the school lobby. At six-three, and well-muscled two hundred pounds, give or take an ounce, he was an imposing figure standing next to the sport trophy case with his arms folded across his chest.

"Good morning," he said in a voice that seemed to echo off the walls. "I've been waiting for you guys. Could we have a word in my office before you start your sessions?"

"Your office?' Ed asked, looking confused. As far as he knew, Chertoff had a broom-closet-sized room off the gym that he used as an office, which was hardly large enough to hold all of them.

"Oh, you haven't heard. The school board has appointed me acting principal until they can make a

decision about a permanent replacement for Douglas."
He turned and walked toward the administrative wing.

They shared puzzled looks as they followed him.

Augusta Peabody sat in her usual place in the outer
office. She smiled at them as they entered, although,
her face tightened a bit when she made eye contact
with Ed.

Inside the principal's office, now empty of all the
photos of Sotheby with various politicians and local
celebrities, and his various awards and honors,
Chertoff plopped himself in the big executive chair
behind the big desk and leaned back casually. Looking
at them. He was the polar opposite of Sotheby. Instead
of an expensive suit with sharply-creased trousers, he
wore his usual khaki pants and polo shirt. He wore
Nike running shoes instead of Sotheby's trademark
highly-polished black wingtips. The most significant
difference, though, was that he was smiling at them
with that loop, open-mouthed, gap-toothed grin that
he always wore during sporting events, which Vernon
Heights seemed to always win, which was a welcome
change from Sotheby's icy, down-his-nose stare as if
you were a particularly noxious specimen in biology
lab.

Once they were seated, Ed cleared his throat. "Uh,
congratulations on the promotion . . . Principal
Chertoff," he said. "Do you think the school board will
make it permanent?"

Chertoff smiled and held up a meaty hand, fingers
crossed.

"Well, I *am* in the running, and I think I have a
good chance," he said. "We'll just have to wait and see.
In the meantime, I just wanted to let you volunteers

know of my appointment, and to thank you for helping us out. Keep up the good work."

He felt a twinge of guilt, but Ed saw an opening. "We're more than happy to help. There is, though, one thing I'd like to ask you to do for us, well, for me."

Chertoff's face turned serious. He leaned forward. "If I can, what is it?"

Ed explained about Joseph Garcia's problem, and his suspicion that the boy suffered from dyslexia. "He's already responded to the picture cards I got for him, but I think he'd benefit from a more structured program."

"You're probably right," Chertoff said. "I'll make arrangements for him to be evaluated right away. We might have to set up an individualized learning program for him next year if you're right and he is dyslexic."

"You mean, you won't hold him back a year?"

"Not without having him evaluated first," Chertoff said, a shocked look on his face. "Before we make a potentially life-altering decision like that, we have to make sure it's the proper one."

Ed felt relieved. At least one good thing had come out of this tragedy.

"Thank you," he said. "And, I know Joseph and his family thank you too."

"No; thank you for bringing this to my attention." He looked at his watch. "Ah, I see it's 9:20. Almost time for your sessions to start. Don't let me keep you. I just wanted to introduce myself and thank you for your service."

Dismissed, they walked back toward the classrooms. Ed's step was buoyant, the police considering him a potential suspect in Sotheby's murder not bothering him for the moment as he exulted in the new situation for his young charge.

"Chertoff is such a breath of fresh air compared to Sotheby, don't you think?" he said.

"Yeah, he's not nearly the stuffed shirt that guy Sotheby was," Ernesto said, nodding in agreement.

Always grounded in reality, Violet ended their kumbaya moment. "Let's not forget, people, we still have a murderer to catch."

Although her reminder knocked a bit of the shine off his ebullient mood, Ed still managed to have a nice morning. Joseph was showing even greater progress with the flash cards, unable to recognize only a few words, and when Ed informed him that the new acting principal had agreed to have him tested and had promised that he wouldn't be held back, he jumped up, ran around the desk, and threw his arms around Ed's neck.

"Thank you, Mr. Ed," he said. "You are my best friend in the whole world."

At the end of the session, Joseph once again hugged Ed and thanked him. This brought back a lot of Ed's positive mood, which was a good thing, because he still had to ride shotgun as Violet drove them home.

He breathed a deep sigh of relief when Violet pulled into the driveway at her house and turned off the ignition, a gesture that she didn't fail to notice.

"If you don't like my driving, Ed Lazenby," she said. "You should just say so."

He stopped, turned and looked her directly in the eye. "I don't like your driving, Violet. You make demolition derby drivers look like Go-Kart racers at a kiddy park."

"Hmph," she said. "I should un-invite you to lunch, you old curmudgeon."

"You can't do that, Violet," Rose said. "Besides, he's right. You are an aggressive driver, and I still don't understand why you never get speeding tickets. You're always driving fifteen miles over the limit."

"I'll have you know, I'm an excellent driver. When was the last time I had an accident?"

"That's only because the way you drive causes other drivers to avoid you," Ernesto said. "And, I think you don't get tickets because all the traffic cops in the area know you, and are afraid of you."

Violet raised her chin and sniffed. "I rest my case," she said, and then she turned and entered the house, leaving them standing on the threshold looking puzzled.

"What was that supposed to mean?" Ernesto asked.

"Best not to ask," Ed said.

"Oh, never mind," Rose said. "Let's go in and have some nice ice tea while Violet fixes lunch. We have some new information we'd like to share with you."

In the living room, Ed and Ernesto took their accustomed seats, the easy chairs at opposite ends of the coffee table, leaving the sofa for Rose and Violet. Rose followed her older sister into the kitchen, and returned a few minutes later with three glasses of ice tea on a silver tray. She set the tray down on the coffee table, took a glass of tea and sat on the sofa, at the end nearest Ernesto, Ed noticed. He picked up a glass and took a sip.

"Okay, Rose," he said after putting his glass down.

"What did you two find out today?"

Rose glanced quickly toward the kitchen. "Well, Violet wanted to be the one to tell you, but she's busy, and it's not fair to keep you waiting. We heard some juicy gossip about the acting principal."

"William Chertoff? What could the coach be up to, shaving points in games or something?"

"No, something even juicier than that."

"What could be worse than cheating?" Ernesto asked.

Rose pouted and glared at him. "Oh, you men. You think sports are the most important thing in the world. Well, let me tell you something Ernesto Cardoza, there are many things that are far more important than sports."

"Okay, you're right, Rose," Ed said, to forestall an argument. "What did you find out about Chertoff?"

"The English teacher said he was thinking about moving to another school. He'd apparently applied for a principal job at a school in western Montgomery County. Now that Sotheby's gone, it's rumored that he's applied for the position at Vernon Heights."

"Interesting," Ed said. "But, it hardly qualifies as a motive for murder."

Rose smiled and lifted her glass to the tip of her nose as if sniffing it. "True, but we heard something else that might. It seems that Mr. Chertoff was sweet on a certain teacher, and she rejected him."

Ed was about to say, 'big deal,' when a thought struck him. "That teacher he was sweet on wouldn't happen to be Helen Wheeler, would it?"

She put the glass down and glared at him. "Oh, Ed, you spoiled it. I wanted to tell you that."

"Sorry, but the way you were going, that seemed the logical answer. So, Chertoff was sweet on Wheeler, but Wheeler rejected him in favor of Sotheby. Now, *there's* a motive for you, one of the oldest in the books. Get rid of your competition, and the way's clear." He snapped his fingers. "In fact, when you think about it, he got rid of his competition for two things—the woman and the job."

"The plot thickens," Ernesto said, rubbing his hands together in a theatrical gesture. "So, how many suspects does that give us, Ed?"

Ed held up a hand, and counted off on his fingers, "Well, we have Augusta Peabody, motive jealousy; Thomas Hadley, motive unknown, but access to the murder weapon; and William Chertoff, motive, jealousy and job. That's three people with either motive or method, and they all had the opportunity."

Rose and Ernesto shared a look and then turned to Ed. "Okay, fearless leader," Ernesto said. "What's our next move?"

"First, we eat lunch," Ed said. "Then, I'll think of something. I don't think too well on an empty stomach."

"Whoa," Violet said. "Before we eat; Ed, what did you learn from Helen Wheeler?"

Ed's mouth dropped open, and then snapped shut. "Uh, I completely forgot to talk to her."

"I kind of figured you would." Violet looked at him with a vulpine grin. "That's why I cornered her in her classroom right after my tutoring session ended."

"Hey, sorry," Ed said. "I was so excited by my young charge's progress with the reading cards, it slipped my mind. So, what'd you learn?"

"She admitted having a fling with Sotheby, but said it ended almost two weeks ago."

"Was she upset over that?"

"Hard to say. I'm not even sure she was telling me the truth about it ending, or when it ended at any rate. I have a hard time telling when people are being truthful."

"You mean, when they're lying, right?" Ed asked.

"No, I mean telling the truth. I assume that most of the time, whenever peoples' lips are moving, they're lying."

Charles Ray

CHAPTER 12

After a lunch of macaroni and cheese, they sat around the dining table, all eyes on Ed. Violet had been a bit put out with Rose for spilling the dirt on Chertoff instead of letting her do it, but by the time they'd finished eating, she was as excited as the rest at having so many people to snoop on.

"Okay, Ed," she said. "What's our next move?"

"Even though I don't think Hadley's our killer, I think we need to find out what it is he's hiding. Rose, you're the kind of person people open up to, so I'm thinking maybe if you just happen to drop by the school this afternoon, you could get him to talk to you, see if you can find out what he's up to."

Rose's head bobbed up and down. "I can do that, no problem."

"What about the rest of us?" Violet asked.

"Hold your water, I'm getting to it," Ed said. "I think you and Ernesto should go talk to the faculty again, see if there are any more relationships or disagreements that might be interesting."

"Aw, why can't I go with Rose," Ernesto said.

"I don't want Hadley to feel ganged up on, Ernesto. Besides, talking to all the faculty would go faster if two of you did it."

Ernesto frowned, but finally nodded his agreement.

"What are you going to do?" Violet asked.

"I am going to kill two birds with one stone . . . I hope. I think I'll drop in on Augusta Peabody and find out how she and her new boss are getting along."

"But, she's a suspect."

"I know that, Violet. But, since I'll be talking to her about someone else, she might not notice if I slip in a few questions that might get at her own motives. Don't worry, I've done stuff like this before. As wacky as it sounds, it works."

Even though she still looked skeptical, Violet nodded. "You're right, it does sound wacky, but it's just wacky enough to work. Okay, when do we leave?"

"As soon as I finish my tea," Ed said.

***

To avoid looking conspicuous, Ed convinced them to use their own cars to go back to the school, and not to park them all together, or all arrive at the same time. He left first, and parked in the first empty slot in the visitor's lot, which also happened to be the first slot, and the closest to the school building. He knew that Ernesto, seeing his Toyota 4-Runner, would park farther in the lot, and Violet, being Violet, would probably park in the faculty parking lot.

Lunch and recess was over, and the students were all in class, so the front of the building was empty and quiet when Ed entered. The long hallway of the administrative wing was also quiet, and somehow different. It took Ed a few moments to realize what had changed—all of the photographs with Douglas Sotheby in them had been removed. Some had been replaced with photos of school events, not featuring anyone in particular, and where they had not been replaced, a light rectangle showed on the wall where the old photo had hung. *Chertoff is cleaning house*, Ed thought wryly. To the man's credit, though, he hadn't replaced Sotheby's photos with his own, unless that was what he planned to do to cover those very noticeable light spaces.

Ed was shaking his head in wonder when he entered the outer office, where Augusta Peabody, her hair loose and hanging to her shoulders rather than pulled back in a bun, sat at her desk, pecking at her computer. She looked up, startled, when he walked in.

"Uh, oh, Mr. Lazenby," she said. "Principal Chertoff is not in at the moment. He had to go to the school board office for a meeting."

My luck is running good. I don't have to keep my voice down when I question her. "That's perfectly okay, Ms. Peabody," Ed said. "It's actually you that I came to see anyway."

Her brows rose, then lowered, then curled downward suspiciously. She looked at him through narrowed slits.

"Why on earth would you want to see me?" Her tone wasn't exactly unfriendly, but it wasn't all that friendly either.

"I wanted to talk to you about the late Principal Sotheby. You probably knew him better than anyone else in the school."

Now, the look on her face was one of naked suspicion.

"Why should you want to talk about him?"

This was the point, Ed knew, where he could win

her trust, or blow it completely. He could go two ways; come up with a story, fabricated in large part, to explain his curiosity, or be up front. Knowing how he disliked people trying to play him, he decided to go the latter route.

"Ms. Peabody, er, may I call you Augusta?" She nodded. "Augusta, I'm gonna level with you. The police are treating me as a suspect in your boss's murder. I didn't do it, of course, and I'm trying to find out who else might've had a reason to do him harm to clear my own name."

Her expression changed from suspicion to surprise. "Why would the police suspect you?"

Ed shrugged. "It's just the way their minds work. I was the one who found the body, and they're always suspicious of the first non-cop on the scene, and then there was the matter of an . . . unfortunately remark I made about him a couple of days before he . . . died."

"What remark? To whom?"

He told her about his confrontation with Sotheby in the tutoring session, and what he'd said after his departure, a remark that was overheard by the janitor and reported to the police.

For the first time since he entered the office, her expression softened.

"I can see why you're worried," she said. "But, I don't think that's enough for anyone to build a case on. I mean, it was obvious to me when Helen and I entered the office that you hadn't done it. I just reacted viscerally at the time, but having had time to think about it, I realize that if you'd done it, you would've been covered in blood."

"Well, thank you for that, Augusta. That'll be very

helpful if the police decide to go down that path. But, I'd still like to know who really did it; just for my own peace of mind."

She leaned forward, pointing a bony finger at him. "You know that you could get in trouble with the police if they find out you're snooping in a case when you're a suspect, don't you?"

"Yes, I know." Ed shrugged. "But, I can't just sit back and do nothing. I already know of three people who might've wanted Sotheby to come to harm, and from what I'm finding out about the man, I suspect there might be others. He wasn't very popular among the faculty here, was he?"

"Well, except for one, you're right about that. But, I don't think anyone on the staff disliked him enough to want to kill him."

"What about the janitor? It was his tool that was used."

"Tom, no, Tom's harmless. You might not have noticed, but he's usually too drunk to do anything more vigorous than push a broom or clip a hedge."

"Drunk? As in drinking on the job?"

"Yes. Tom Hadley is what I think people call a high-functioning alcoholic. He's okay as long as he has his alcohol. You'd only ever know he was a drunk if he was cut off from it."

"Did Sotheby know this?"

"Of course, he knew. You see, Douglas Sotheby was a recovering alcoholic himself, so he decided to give Tom a chance to get his act together."

"Isn't it possible that he put pressure on him because he was still drinking?"

She shook her head. "No. He knew Tom was still

drinking, but he's cutting back bit by bit, and Douglas, Principal Sotheby, knew that pushing him could destroy what progress was being made. Besides, he's just a janitor, his drinking doesn't really threaten anything critical. It's not like he's a bus driver, or has contact with students."

Ed decided to play what he thought was his trump card, Chertoff's frustrated relationship with Wheeler.

"What about the new acting principal? I heard a rumor that Mr. Chertoff has a thing for Helen Wheeler, and she'd turned him down and was having an affair with Sotheby. Do you think he would want Chertoff hurt?"

"Over Helen, I doubt it. William might be a football coach, but in reality, he's just a pussycat. Besides, Douglas was about to break off that relationship. I overheard him and Helen arguing a few days before he was killed, saying that he was afraid his wife might find out, and he didn't need the grief."

Oh my, Ed thought, that adds Wheeler to the list of possible suspects.

"So, she might've done it?"

"I don't think so, but Helen can have a fiery temper. If you want to know someone who had it in for him, and who I think is perfectly capable of killing someone, you shouldn't look at faculty, you should be looking at parents."

"Parent? Which parent are you referring to?"

"A man named Wilton Fish," she said. "Douglas was about to expel his son for fighting, and Mr. Fish blew his fuse about it; just the day before he was killed."

"Did you tell the police about this incident?"

Her mouth made a little round 'o.' "Oh, my

goodness," she said. "When they talked to me, they only asked about members of the faculty. That incident slipped my mind. I should call them, shouldn't I?"

"It's up to you, but if I were you, I wouldn't tell them it was in a conversation with me that you remembered. They might think we were colluding or something."

"Don't worry, I'll wait a day or two, just in case someone noticed you visiting me today. So, what will you do now?"

Ed hated jumping to hasty conclusions, but he'd also learned over the years to trust his instincts about people. And, just as his instincts had told him that Thomas Hadley wasn't the killer, they were fairly shouting at him now that this prim-looking, often up-tight woman sitting behind her desk looking up at him with a kind smile was innocent as well. His gut told him that she was someone he could trust. Hoping this wasn't the first time his gut let him down, he decided to go all in. "I think I need to have a talk with Mr. Fish. Can you get me his address?"

Her smile broadened.

"I certainly can." She hit some keys on her computer keyboard. The screen lit up, and she punched a few more keys, peering down at the screen. From where he stood, Ed couldn't make out what was there, but it must've been what she sought, because she picked up a pen and a notepad and scribbled something. She then tore the sheet she'd written on from the pad, and held it up for Ed. "Here's his home address and phone number."

"Thanks, Augusta," Ed said, taking the paper from

her, folding it, and stuffing it into his shirt pocket. "You've been a big help."

"My pleasure, Ed," she said. "You be careful. This man, Milton Fish, is big and mean."

Ed looked down at her, his brow furrowed and his gaze intent. "I'm not so big, but I can be pretty mean myself."

"Ooh, I'll just bet you can." Her cheeks turned red.

Ed was halfway back to the entry lobby before he realized that her demeanor toward him had completely changed during the course of their conversation, and at the end she was . . . really friendly to the point of almost flirting. He shook his head, thinking that he had to be reading more into it than was actually there. Besides, he had to come up with an excuse for talking to Milton Fish without arousing suspicion.

CHAPTER 13

The Fish residence was a small, one story, tract-style house in a modest, middle class housing community, on Muncaster Mill Road in the north part of Rockville. Developed in the early 1980s, just as the local housing boom was starting, Potomac Hill didn't have the variety of housing types that had come to typify housing developments in the DC area once the boom got underway. The builder had simply stamped out 250 rectangular dwellings, mostly one-story, that looked like the cookie-cutter housing projects of the 1950s, differing only in the color of the roof slates or siding. Priced in the low two-hundred thousands, they were occupied by low-level white-collar types, mechanics, and other blue-collar workers lucky enough to be making more than minimum wage – not a wealthy community, but not the working poor either.

When Ed turned off Muncaster Mill onto Potomac Drive, the community's main street, he noticed a lot of on-street parking, and a lot of pickups, one of the first signs that a community is being de-gentrified, something that was happening more and more as those in the upper middle class took out outrageously expensive mortgages to move into the newer communities with Cape Cods, Colonials, and other up-scale-looking styles of houses.

He saw no cars in front of, or in the driveway, of the house, and wondered if perhaps this was a two-person working family, with no one at home in the middle of the afternoon. He pulled his Toyota 4-Runner to the curb directly in front of the house and killed the engine. For a few minutes, he sat there looking around. The sidewalks were empty, and a cursory glance didn't reveal the movement of curtains indicating that someone was watching his arrival. After driving all the way there, though, he figured that he might as well check it out, so he unbuckled his seatbelt and got out. After another look around, he walked up the driveway and then followed the flagstone walk to the front door.

A deep, grandfather-clock-like sound followed his pushing of the doorbell button. After a few seconds, he heard the sound of footsteps from inside. So, someone was home.

The door swung inward, revealing a woman about three inches shorter than his own five-eleven, but probably forty pounds heavier than his hundred-ninety pounds. She had a pudgy face, ruddy cheeks, and tiny brown eyes beneath a single, dark brown brow over her nose like some hairy caterpillar. It reminded Ed of a cartoon character, and he had to bite back a grin. Her pinched lips were unsmiling.

"We ain't buyin' nothin' today," she said in a squeaky voice, further reinforcing the cartoon character image, and almost defeating his control over his desire to laugh.

"I'm not selling anything, ma'am," Ed said. "Is this the Fish residence?"

"Yeah, it is. Whaddya want?" Her tone was

suspicious and unfriendly.

"I'd like to speak to your husband if he's home."

"He ain't home," she said, verifying Ed's guess that she was Mrs. Fish.

"Can you tell me how I can get in touch with him, please. It's very important that I speak with him."

"What about?"

Ed mentally crossed his fingers. He didn't like lying, even small lies, but, if this Fish character was a viable suspect, he didn't want him alerted. "My name's Ed Lazenby, ma'am, and I work at Vernon Heights Middle School. I need to talk to your husband about your son's schoolwork."

Her look of suspicion deepened. "I'm his mama, why can't you talk to me?"

Now, Ed knew he was on shaky ground, but he was committed. Peabody hadn't mentioned the boy's mother being at the meeting between Fish and Sotheby, though, so he took a chance.

"Well, ma'am, it's about your husband's meeting with the principal last week. There were some issues that he might not have fully understood, so I've been asked to meet with him to clear them up."

"You mean 'bout our boy gettin' expelled?" The suspicion had turned to anger, and her pink cheeks turned red.

"Uh, yes ma'am. I think there might've been a misunderstanding on that point."

"You mean he ain't gonna get expelled?"

"That's quite possible." *Lord, forgive me for breaking the Commandment about lying.* "I need to clarify a few things with your husband, though, to make sure the misunderstanding is cleared up."

Her expression softened, from hot anger to only glacial hostility.

"Well, it's 'bout time. My old man's at work right now. He don't get home until 'round 7:00."

Darn it, Ed thought, I should've asked Peabody for a work address as well.

"Can you give me the address of where he works? I'll drive there and talk to him."

He thought he saw another flicker of suspicion in her eyes, and feared that she would challenge him for not knowing that, but then it passed.

"He's at his garage on Georgia Avenue, Fish's Fix-up. You can't miss it, it's at the corner of Georgia and Randolph Road. But, you better be talkin' fast to him, 'cause he's steamed at that principal of yours for threatenin' to throw our boy out of school."

"Thank you for your time, Mrs. Fish," Ed said, and began making a hasty retreat toward his car before she could think about his ignorance of Fish's business address, which was probably part of the school records.

As he fastened his seatbelt and started the engine, he glanced out of the corner of his eye, and saw her bulk still standing in the doorway glaring at him.

Because of the afternoon traffic, and school buses that always seemed to have multiple stops to disgorge students whenever he was behind them, it took him half an hour to get to Milton Fish's place of business. It looked like every other garage in the area, a large gravel-covered lot littered with cars and trucks in various stages of disassembly or damage, in the center of which stood a large metal building with huge sliding doors in front a small door to the right and small windows on both sides of the doors. A line of relatively undamaged pickup trucks and a small Honda Civic near the building indicated a possible parking area, so Ed pulled in at the end of the line, next to the Honda, and got out.

The noise was audible outside, but when he pulled the door open and stepped inside, the volume of noise almost knocked him off his feet. He clapped his hands over his ears, which only helped a little, He could still feel the vibrations in his skull.

There were six vehicles, five cars and a pickup, being worked on inside the building. The pickup and three cars were on raised platforms and two cars were over pits. Two men, large, muscular men wearing grease-stained coveralls, worked on the truck. Each car had one man working on it. The main noise came from an electric sander that one man was using to strip the paint from a car that was missing all its doors, and another who was using a pneumatic hammer under another car. Between the shriek of the sander and the booming sound of the hammer, Ed quickly felt the beginnings of a headache. He wondered how anyone could work in such a din, until he noticed that all the men were wearing large earmuffs that covered their ears and part of their cheeks.

In the far corner of the space was an enclosed office with a ceiling to hip-high window spanning one wall, giving a clear view from inside, and of the inside. It was empty, so Ed assumed that one of the seven men working on vehicles was Milton Fish.

As he walked along the line of vehicles, peeking into the pits, which were nearest to the door, and up at the men perched on the raised platforms, he realized that he had no idea what Fish looked like. Then, when he came to the pickup, he noticed that one of the two men working on it was much larger than the other, with shoulders at least three feet wide, a gut that made it difficult for him to lean over to work under the raised hood, and a mean-looking snarl on his greasy face.

Now, of course, he had a problem. How to get Fish's attention in all that noise. Shouting was out, and he wasn't about to climb upon the hoist. So, he opted for the simplest solution; he walked over to the hoist, and tapped on the man's work boots.

At his touch, the big man jerked erect, bumping his head on the hood of the truck, and almost falling backwards off the platform, only avoiding a nasty tumble by grabbing the edge of the engine compartment. He turned, and looked down. When he saw Ed standing there, his face twisted into a flaming rage. His mouth was working, but Ed couldn't make out his words under the noise. He tapped his ears and shook his head.

With surprising agility for his size, the big man jumped off the hoist, landing in a semi-crouch in front of Ed. He poked a large forefinger in Ed's chest, and motioned toward the door with his thumb. The meaning was clear, 'let's go outside.'

Once they were outside and the closed door had muted the noise to a decibel level that permitted conversation, the big man ripped off his ear muffs and glared at Ed. "Who the hell are you, old man, and what are you doing in my workshop? Don't you know better'n to surprise a man working under the hood of a truck like that?"

Ed shrank back under the verbal assault, holding his hands up in a placating gesture.

"Sorry, but with all the noise, I couldn't think of any other way to get your attention," he said. "Are you Milton Fish?"

"Yeah, I am. Who the fuck wants to know?"

The man towered over Ed, and as he stood there, his face contorted in anger and his hands—even the one holding the ear muffs—clenched in fists, he could understand why his son was in danger of being expelled for fighting. A surly mother and a father who seemed willing to fight at the drop of a dime would do that to a kid, he thought.

"My name's Ed Lazenby, I'm a volunteer tutor at Vernon Heights, and I wanted to talk to you about your son."

The look on the man's face darkened, and the muscles in his jaw tensed. "Has Skeeter been fightin' again? Dammit, I'm gonna whup that little punk within an inch of his life when I get home."

"No, no, it's not that. As far as I know, your son hasn't been involved in any altercations lately." Ed hoped that was true. "But, I would like to talk to you about your last meeting with Principal Sotheby."

Some of the tension went out of Fish's jaw, but only a little.

"Why would you wanna know that? If you work at the school, you should already know."

"Well," Ed said. "I know that you had a bit of a disagreement after the principal said he was considering expelling your son for fighting."

"Yeah, I guess you could call it a . . . bit of a disagreement. I told that sumbitch I'd rip his head off if he threw my boy outa school."

"That's harsh, don't you think?"

Fish laughed, but there was no mirth in it. "Aw, I wouldn't actually rip the fucker's head off, I'd just pound on him a little 'til he come to his senses and made the right decision, know what I mean."

"You know it's a crime to threaten someone like that."

"I'd like to see him prove I threatened him. He call the cops on me, and I'll sue his ass."

Ed pulled up short mentally on that. It didn't appear that Fish knew that Sotheby was dead. But, given that it was all over the local TV news, and had made the front page of the local section in the *Washington Post*, Ed found that hard to believe. The man didn't look all that bright, but Ed wondered if he was putting on an act. He decided to test it.

"Would you be willing to have another meeting with the principal to discuss the issue?"

"Did he finally make up his mind?"

"Huh? Come again?" Now, Ed was confused. He didn't sense the man was being evasive. In fact, he seemed as confused as Ed.

"Well, I mean, he didn't actually say he was gonna expel Skeeter, just that it was one of the things he was considerin', you know. When he said that, I kinda blew a fuse, you see, and he asked me to leave, so I left. If I'd stayed, I mighta popped in that arrogant face of his. Anyway, if he's ready to be reasonable, I'll come talk to him, but if he starts that shit about throwin' my boy outa school, I *am* gonna bust his face."

"Oh, well, that puts a different light on things."

"Whatcha mean? When do I gotta go see this

turkey?"

"Ah, well, I'll get back to you on that."

Ed turned and headed for his car. Like his wife, Fish just stood there, watching him through narrow slits. *Darn, he really doesn't know Sotheby's dead. I guess he and his wife only watch Fox News, and missed that story, or maybe they don't watch the news at all. I need to talk to Augusta again.*

Charles Ray

CHAPTER 14

Georgia Avenue was choked with northbound rush hour traffic, and it took Ed an hour to get back to PVC. His nerves were frazzled from the rudeness and mindlessness of rush-hour commuters by the time he pulled into the gate at PVC. The guard on duty recognized him, and just waved him through, which was a good thing. Another setback, like being stopped by a guard who'd seen him and his car every day, would've snapped the last thread of calm he possessed. All he wanted to do was get home, put some ice cubes in a glass, cover them with a large dollop of Jim Beam, and begin to drink himself to oblivion.

Of course, he knew he wouldn't really do that. He seldom drank to the point of inebriation, except when he and Ernesto were playing dominos or talking about old times and he lost track of the number of drinks they'd had. The thought of the hangovers experienced about once a month, made him think it might be better to make a pitcher of lemonade instead. He could always spike it with a shot glass or two of vodka for a little kick.

When he pulled into his driveway, Ernesto came out of his house and trotted across the street.

"Hey, man, I been waiting for you to get home.

How'd it go with Peabody?"

"Come on inside, and I'll tell you while I squeeze some lemons."

"You gonna squeeze a little vodka in with 'em?"

"Maybe more than just a little."

"Your day was that good, eh?"

"I'm not saying a thing until I've drunk half a glass of lemonade," Ed said.

Ernesto did a lip-zipping gesture and followed him into the house. Although he remained silent, he followed Ed into the kitchen, hovering nearby as Ed squeezed a dozen lemons into a pitcher, added sugar and water, and stirred. He said nothing as Ed took ice cubes from the icemaker in his refrigerator and put them in an aluminum ice bucket. And, he was mute as Ed put the bucket of ice and the pitcher of lemonade, along with four tumblers, onto a plastic tray which he carried to the living room, where he put it on the coffee table. His mouth stayed shut while Ed took a bottle of vodka and a bottle of tequila from his liquor cabinet and placed them next to the tray on the coffee table, and he silently toasted with Ed after he'd half-filled two glasses with lemonade and handed him one.

After downing the contents of the glass, Ernesto wiped his lips and then made an unzipping gesture.

"Okay, we can talk now, right?" he said.

Ed put his glass down and wiped his lips. "Sure, but let's drink while we talk."

He poured more lemonade into their glasses, and then pointed at the two bottles of fiery liquor.

"Let's start with the tequila," Ernesto said.

Ed poured a healthy amount of the oily liquor into each glass. They hoisted glasses, toasted again, and took long swallows.

After wiping his mouth and belching loudly, Ed sat back.

"Okay, here's how my day went," he said. He then went on to describe his meetings with Augusta Peabody and Milton Fish.

"Sounds like you're ruling them out as suspects," Ernesto said when he'd finished.

"Yeah. I just didn't get any guilty vibes from Augusta when I talked to her," Ed said. "As for Fish, he didn't even seem to know that Sotheby was dead."

Ernesto looked surprised. "How can that be? It was all over the news."

Ed took another sip from his glass.

"If you'd met this guy and his wife, you'd understand. I got the sense that she doesn't even know what's going on in her neighborhood. As for him, he's a big bully who probably only reads the sports page, if he reads at all, and I doubt he watches the evening news on TV."

"Damn, Ed, who does that leave us with?"

"Well, I'm not ruling either of them out entirely, just putting them at the bottom of my list." He stood and walked across to the credenza. After taking a notepad and ballpoint from the top drawer, he returned to the sofa. He opened the notepad, and began writing. "Here are the suspects as I see them now," he said.

On the pad, he wrote,

Thomas Hadley
William Chertoff
Augusta Peabody
Milton Fish

Helen Wheeler

When Ernesto saw the last name, he leaned forward and stabbed it with his finger. "Why did you put Helen Wheeler's name on the list?"

"According to Augusta, Sotheby was breaking off their relationship, and Helen didn't take it too well. Her motive would be anger at being scorned."

"That's really reaching, amigo. Besides, Augusta could be lying, you know."

"I know, and even though I didn't get the sense that she was lying, that's why her name's still on the list. Same thing with Fish. Hell, he could be one of those pathological liars, and I wouldn't be able to read him."

"Why do you have Hadley's name at the top of the list? I thought you said you didn't think he did it."

"I don't," Ed said. "But, Augusta said he's an alcoholic, so my read of him might be off. He *is* hiding something, and if I could find out what that is, I might be able to get a more accurate reading."

Ernesto shook his head. "Five suspects, all with motives, and as far as we know, opportunity. Hadley's the main one with access to the murder weapon, so for my money, he belongs at the top of the list."

"You're right, but something about it doesn't feel right."

"What?"

"I don't know, Ernesto. Just a gut feeling I have that we're missing something."

The phone rang. Ed picked it up on the third ring. "Hello," he said.

"Ed, glad I caught you home," Janzen's voice said. Ed detected a note of tension in it.

"What's up, Carl?"

Janzen didn't respond right away. When he did, his voice was low, and the worry in his voice was clear.

"Look, I shouldn't even be telling you this, but . . . well, I think they're wrong, and I didn't want you blindsided."

"What? Who? Carl, what're you talking about?"

"Jefferson and Wayne talked to the boss. They're looking at you as the prime suspect. They got his permission to interrogate you."

Ed didn't like that word. Interrogate. Not question, or talk to, but interrogate. That sounded so serious, and while he knew he was innocent and had nothing to had, he still felt an emptiness in the pit of his stomach.

"Well, I'm right here," he said, as calmly as he was able. "They can come by anytime."

"You don't understand, Ed," Janzen said. "They're not coming to your place. They plan to bring you in to the station and do it."

Shit, Ed thought, now, *that is* serious.

"When?" he asked.

"I don't know, but I figure they won't waste any time. You should get yourself a good lawyer for this."

"You might be right, but I didn't do anything, so that might send the wrong signal, don't you think?"

"Wrong signal or not, you need to make sure you get the best possible legal advice. Believe me, if they have their sights set on you, they'll pull out all the stops to get you to confess. A wrong answer could land you in deep shit. A lawyer's the best way to avoid that."

Ed knew that he was right, but it didn't feel right.

Innocent people shouldn't need lawyers, and he was innocent, dammit.

"I'll think about it," he said.

"Okay, I hope you make the right decision." Janzen broke the connection.

So do I. But, before he could think further about it, the phone rang again. "Lazenby residence," he said.

"Mr. Lazenby, this is Detective Aubrey Jefferson," the gruff voice in ear said. "We need you to come down to the station. We have a few more questions for you about the Sotheby murder." He gave Ed the address, and told him that the desk sergeant would be expecting him as soon as possible.

When he hung up the phone, Ed turned to Ernesto, who had been sitting quietly on the sofa, looking on and listening to Ed's side of the conversation with a worried look on his face.

Putting on as calm a face as he could manage, Ed said, "I have to go to police headquarters to talk to the detectives. I think I need to brush my teeth and gargle first, though. Wouldn't do to have them smell tequila on my breath."

CHAPTER 15

The Montgomery County Police Department Investigation Division is located in Gaithersburg, just off Darnestown Road, or US 28, west of Rockville, in a multi-story, academic-looking building, on scenic acreage that includes a large lake fronting the building. Once the home of the National Geographic Society, which moved its headquarters into the District of Columbia, it looks like anything but a police headquarters.

Its location, though, required Ed to drive across Rockville, cross I-270, and make his way with fairly heavy traffic to Edison Park Drive, a winding, two-lane asphalt road that wound past the east side of the building to several tree-lined parking lots in back. In the visitors' lot, Ed found a parking space in the very back, leaving him a long walk across the macadam to the public entrance.

As Jefferson promised, the desk sergeant, seated behind a large wooden desk on an elevated platform, was expecting him. When he gave his name, the uniformed officer had him sign a register, gave him a VISITOR pass, and told him to have a seat in the waiting area until someone came to escort him to the Investigation Division. The plastic chairs, arranged in rows like school desks, all facing the desk sergeant, weren't designed for comfort, although the drunk or doped up young man draped across one in the row behind where Ed sat didn't seem to mind. He sat there for what seemed like an eternity, watching the comings and goings of people who had business with the police department, mostly those in trouble, and waited for the 'someone' who was to escort him to Detective Jefferson.

That someone turned out to be Jefferson himself. He looked rumpled, and the dark bags under his eyes indicated he hadn't been sleeping well.

He stopped in front of Ed, looking down at him with bloodshot eyes. "Thanks for coming on such short notice, Mr. Lazenby," he said. "Why don't you come with me." Without waiting for Ed to respond, he turned and began walking toward the back of the big entrance lobby to a row of elevator doors.

Ed rose and followed, reaching him just as an elevator door whooshed open and two uniformed officers with a staggering, mumbling man between them stepped out. Jefferson stepped aside and motioned for Ed to precede him into the elevator, then stepped in behind him and stabbed at a button on the control panel.

The elevator only went up two floors, but it seemed to Ed that it took forever. Jefferson said nothing to him the entire time. He just stood there looking at a spot on the elevator wall over Ed's left shoulder, seemingly lost in thought. When the elevator came to a jerky stop, it caught Ed by surprise, and he grasped the safety rail in reflex. Jefferson stepped out and stood there waiting for him to exit. When he did, the detective turned and walked through a vast space with paired desks scattered about in a haphazard manner. People, mostly men, sat behind the desks, either talking to the person at the desk facing them, on the phone, typing on laptop computers, or talking to dejected-looking people sitting in the lone chair to the right of each desk. Ed noticed that a good number of the people sitting in the chairs were wearing handcuffs, and he wondered if that's what Jefferson had in mind for him.

His unasked question was answered when they reached the end of the area at a hallway with two doors on either side. A sign above the entrance to the hallway read, INTERVIEW AREA.

"We're in the second room on the right," Jefferson said. He moved in front of Ed, opened the door and stood aside to allow Ed to enter.

The room was sparsely furnished and bleak. Gray walls with a large mirror in the wall facing the door, a wooden table in the center, and three chairs, one to the left and two to the right. Detective Sheldon Wayne, a scowl on his dark face, sat in one of the two chairs. He looked up as Ed entered, and his scowl deepened. On the table was a tape recorder and a microphone. The microphone pointed to the single chair. Ed stood, awaiting instructions, even though he had a pretty good idea where he was supposed to sit.

Jefferson pointed at the lone chair. "Have a seat, Mr. Lazenby."

Ed sat and folded his hands in his lap. He returned Wayne's scowl with a calm expression, refusing to break eye contact. *I'm familiar with that tactic. Try to intimidate me from the get-go. Well, that's not gonna work with me.*

Jefferson took the empty chair next to his partner. His face was as calm as Ed's, not friendly, but not attempting to assert dominance.

Ah ha, they're gonna pull the good cop, bad cop routine. Now, Ed was beginning to feel a tinge of anger. *Well, bring it on.*

"We'll be recording this interview, Mr. Lazenby," Jefferson said. "Do you have any objections?"

"No." Ed didn't need a lawyer to tell him to keep his answers short and to the point.

Jefferson pushed the power button, and a green light on the side of the machine blinked on.

"Detective First Grade Aubrey Jefferson and Detective Sheldon Wayne interviewing Mr. . . . your name's Edward, right?" Ed nodded. "Interviewing Mr. Edward Lazenby." He turned to his partner and nodded.

"Mr. Lazenby, you have the right to remain silent and not answer questions. However, if you give up that right, anything you say can and will be used against you in a court of law. You have the right to have an attorney present during questioning. If you can't afford an attorney, one will be appointed for you. Do you understand these rights?"

"I do."

"Do you wish to have an attorney present?"

"No."

"The . . . Mr. Lazenby has declined to have an attorney present," he said, and sat back, folding his arms across his chest.

"Mr. Lazenby," Jefferson said. "We've asked you here to do a follow up interview regarding the . . . death of one Douglas Southeby Friday before last. I realize that you've already made a statement, but just for the record, would you please walk us through what happened?"

In a calm voice, Ed described arriving at school with Ernesto and starting for his class, but because he was early, decided that he would first talk to Sotheby about getting Joseph Garcia tested for dyslexia. "When I arrived at his office, his secretary was out, but the door to his office was ajar, so I went in, and that's when I found him. He appeared to be dead."

"Appeared to be dead?" Wayne said. "Why appeared to be dead?"

"I'm not a doctor, but, he had a pair of pruning shears stuck in his chest, blood all over the front of his clothes, and blood on the desk. I assumed he was dead."

"What happened next?"

"Then, Augusta Peabody, his secretary, and Helen Wheeler, a teacher, came into the office. They were a bit shook up, so after I calmed them down and got them out of the office, I called 911 and reported it."

"How long had you been in Sotheby's office before the two women came in?" Jefferson asked.

"I can't be sure, but not more than a minute or two."

"You sure it couldn't have been longer?" Wayne asked. "Say, five or ten minutes?"

"I'm sure."

The black detective looked at Ed with an expression of frustration. "Okay, let's talk about your relationship with the deceased."

"He was the principal of the school, and I'm a volunteer tutor."

"Did you two get along?"

"We disagreed on whether or not the Garcia boy has dyslexia or is just a slow learner," Ed said. "Other than that, the only other time I ever saw him—other than when I found him dead—was during orientation."

"That's not really answering my question, Lazenby."

"We disagreed on one thing. Other than that, we *had* no relationship, so I can't say that we did or didn't get along."

"You tryin' to be funny?" He leaned forward, his fists pressed into the tabletop.

Jefferson laid a hand on his partner's arm. "Take it easy, Milt. I understand what Mr. Lazenby's sayin'. He didn't really know the victim all that well. Is that about right, Mr. Lazenby?"

"That's correct."

Wayne, though, was not quite done. "Isn't true, *Mr.* Lazenby, that you threatened the victim?"

"I made an unfortunate comment about him, but, he wasn't present at the time, so it was hardly a threat."

"You said you'd like to put his lights out, right? Called him a turkey?"

Ed hesitated before answering, then decided that since they already knew that he'd said it—he'd admitted to it at the scene when they brought it up—he needed to provide some context.

"Yes, I said that. I was muttering to myself, though, out of frustration over his obstinacy, not as an actual threat. And, the fact is, he was a turkey." Then, realizing that he was saying too much, Ed snapped his lips shut.

Wayne slammed his hand on the table, causing Ed

to flinch. "And, why should I believe you?" Spittle flew from his mouth. "Why do you say he was a turkey?"

Ed took a deep breath, still maintaining eye contact. "Because, it's the truth," he said. "He was considering holding a child back without having him tested first to see what the true problem was. Enough to upset me, but hardly a motive to murder someone."

Jefferson was sitting back in his chair, his gaze going from his partner to Ed, his expression unreadable.

"Did you kill Douglas Southeby?" Wayne asked.

"No, I did not."

"Prove it!"

Ed almost smiled. The man was desperate, and he either thought Ed was ignorant of the law, or was baiting him. He decided to go with the latter.

"When you arrived, did you see any blood on me, or my clothing?"

Wayne blinked. Ed thought he saw the flicker of a smile on Jefferson's face.

"No, but you could've cleaned up before we arrived."

"Right," Ed said. "I took a change of clothing with me when I went to tutor that day. Where did I put the clothing I took off? Did you find anything?"

Wayne shook his head. "No, we didn't, but that means nothing. You could've stabbed the victim from behind. No blood would've spattered on you then."

Now, Ed smiled.

"Right, Sotheby and I had only known each other for a few days, and as you know, we didn't agree on the child I was tutoring. So, do you really believe he'd let me walk around his desk and get behind him with pruning shears in my hand, and even if I'd stabbed him from behind, blood would've gotten on my sleeves. Oh, and how did I get those shears, by the way?"

"The janitor said his tools were outside the shed that morning, and just before the body was discovered he noticed that his shears were missing. You could've taken them."

"I'm assuming you've talked to Ernesto Cardoza," Ed said. "He and I came in together that morning. He can attest that I didn't take those shears."

Wayne didn't look convinced. "Yeah, we talked to him, but you could've gone back outside after you two separated and done it."

"And, just how did I get back inside the school carrying a pair of pruning shears without someone noticing, and how am I supposed to have gotten out of Sotheby's office in bloody clothing, changed and gone back in without anyone noticing? I'm sorry, detective, but you're making no sense."

"You could've used the back door to the victim's office." Wayne smiled wolfishly.

"What back door?" Ed asked.

The detective's face showed a momentary flicker of surprise, which he quickly brought under control.

"Don't try to tell me you didn't know about Sotheby's private entrance?"

"I didn't, and the only door into his office that I'm aware of is the one behind his secretary's desk."

Now, there was uncertainty on Wayne's face. He looked at his partner.

"I think he's tellin' the truth," Jefferson said.

Wayne turned back and glowered at Ed. "You didn't see the other door?"

"I don't know what you're talking about," Ed said. "I

only saw the door I came through."

Jefferson, sighed and laid a hand on his partner's arm again. "Check it Milt, I think he's tellin' the truth. He doesn't know about Sotheby's secret door."

"He could just be good at concealing things," Wayne said, but there was little conviction in his voice.

Jefferson shook his head.

"Nah, I don't think he's that good." He turned to face Ed. "Mr. Lazenby, I think that's all the questions we have for you today. This interview is concluded." He reached over and switched off the recorder.

Ed sat, looking and feeling confused.

"You can go, Mr. Lazenby," Jefferson said.

"Uh, oh, sure, thanks, detective, but I'm confused. What's this nonsense about another door?"

"Sotheby had a concealed door in his office. It's designed to look like a simple wall panel, but from outside, it's clearly a door. Apparently, he used it to come and go without having to mix with the rest of the school population." A harsh look from Wayne caused him to look embarrassed and stop talking.

Ed had many questions, first among them, 'are you guys still looking at me as a suspect?', but decided it might not be prudent to extend his stay in police headquarters, so he stood. Jefferson also stood.

"I'll escort you downstairs," he said.

"Don't plan on any out of town trips, though," Wayne said to Ed's back as he walked through the door.

Ed left confused. The detectives, Jefferson at least, seemed to believe his version of events. Wayne's hostility he put down to his being frustrated over not having another suspect. The existence of this other door, though, put a different spin on things. That left open the possibility that someone from outside could've done it as easily as someone on the faculty. If, with all their resources, the police were stymied, he and his team of amateur misfits were facing a real hurdle.

CHAPTER 16

Fighting the beginning crush of rush hour traffic meant that it was dark by the time Ed got back home. Ernesto came out of his house when Ed pulled into his driveway. He was at the driver's side of the car, looking curious and excited, before Ed could turn the engine off.

"How'd it go at the cop house?" Ernesto asked.

"About what you'd expect," Ed replied. He described their good cop, bad cop routine, and Wayne's frustration when it didn't work. Then, he told Ernesto about the 'door' in Sotheby's office.

"So, there's a way somebody could've gotten in, killed him, and left, without even being seen by his secretary."

"That's what I'm thinking, but who would know about that door? I suppose Augusta comes to mind, after all, she's his personal secretary, but I just don't see her as a murderer."

Ernesto gave him a funny look. "What about Helen Wheeler? She was shagging him. Maybe she knew about it."

"Good point. We need to check her out. We also need to check Chertoff and Hadley, . . . and, just to be thorough, Augusta as well."

"For a minute there, my friend, I thought you were

going soft on me . . . or soft on Ms. Peabody."

Ed's cheeks felt hot. "Now, why would I be doing that?"

"Hell, you tell me. You talk to her once, and all of a sudden, you're convinced she's innocent."

"Hey, it only takes once. I didn't get the sense she's hiding anything. But, you're right that we need to keep an open mind, so we check her out."

The phone rang. Ed got up and answered it, listened for a few seconds, and then he put his hand over the mouthpiece. "Well, looks like we'll get our chance to check Augusta out sooner than I expected," he said quietly. "She's on the phone, and she wants to come here and talk to me."

Ernesto shrugged. "Okay then, let's do it."

"She said she wanted to talk to me, so I think it might be better if it's *just* me here when she gets here."

"Okay, but you gotta promise to fill me in as soon as she's gone."

"Good," Ed said, and removed his hand from the phone. "Okay, Augusta, come on over. Do you know the address? Good. See you in half an hour."

He hung up. Ernesto smiled. "Well, we have time for one drink before she gets here."

Ed kept him to that promise, and after one whiskey, about two fingers over ice, sent him home. He put on a pot of tea to brew, and sliced some cheese, which he put on a tray with an assortment of salt-free crackers. The tea was just the right shade of brown when his doorbell rang.

Augusta Peabody didn't look like she did in her office. There, she was prim and proper, her hair pulled back severely, and always dressed in monochromatic—

mostly gray or light blue—clothing that didn't show off her figure. The woman who walked into Ed's living room was someone else entirely.

Her dark brown hair hung loose around her head, draping down to her shoulders, and she'd put on a darker lipstick than she normally wore. In the place of her severely cut monochromatic suit, she wore faded jeans that hugged shapely legs, and a man's polo shirt that was straining to hold her generous breasts.

While not an ugly woman, in her daily persona, she was what Ed would call 'easily forgettable,' but the woman standing in his doorway, smiling at the way he gaped at her was anything but forgettable.

"Well, aren't you going to offer me a seat?" she asked in a playful voice.

Ed swallowed hard. "Uh, sorry, where are my manners? Please come in, have a seat. Can I get you something to drink?" He realized that he was rambling, and sounding like a clumsy teen on his first date.

She seemed to take it in stride. She walked past him, and he couldn't help but notice the way her hips moved inside her tight jeans, to the sofa, where she sat, leaned back with her left arm on the arm rest and her legs crossed.

"W-what would you like? I also have some cheese and crackers."

"Cheese and crackers sounds fine," she said. "As for a drink, what do you usually drink?"

"I just had a mild Jim Beam before you arrived, so I'm sticking with whiskey."

She fluttered her lashes at him, an overtly flirtatious gesture that Ed found a bit unsettling—in a nice way. "I'll have Jim Beam, with a little water and ice, if you don't mind."

Trying to control the impact of her appearance and actions, Ed went to the credenza and began mixing their drinks. She was at least twenty years his junior, probably in her late forties if the light webs of crows' feet at the corners of her eyes were any indication. But, rather than making her look old or unattractive, they only added character to her face, which, with her hair down, was pleasant to look at. *Don't forget, she's still a suspect,* he chided himself.

His hands had a slight tremor as he returned to the sofa with the drinks. When she took hers, their fingers grazed, and Ed felt a slight tingle from his fingertips to his elbow.

He raised his glass in a toast to mask the reaction to her touch. "Over the lips and past the gums, look out liver, here it comes," he said.

She giggled. "I didn't know anyone still did those corny toasts. My father used to do that." She clinked her glass against his and then took a sip. "Nice, not too strong, not too weak. It's as if you know my taste in liquor."

"Actually, I don't. But, I always make mine a tad on the weak side. I don't like getting drunk, and I hate hangovers."

"I'm the same way," she said. "I hate that feeling of not being in control."

Ed nodded. Her words mirrored his own reaction to being inebriated.

"Oh, say, I forgot the cheese and crackers," he said. "And, I made a pot of tea. I hope you like tea."

"I love tea." She took another sip of whiskey and then put her glass down. "In fact, I think I'd prefer tea to alcohol . . . if you don't mind."

"No, not at all." He rose. She stood. "Oh, why don't you just make yourself comfortable. I'll go to the kitchen and get the tea and snacks."

"You sure I can't help?"

"You're my guest," Ed said. "Guests don't work in the Lazenby household."

He made a hasty retreat to the kitchen. Before picking up the tray containing the snacks, teapot, cups, and condiments, he paused to catch his breath. *Get yourself together, Ed boy. Sure, she's a fine-looking woman, but until you figure out who killed Sotheby, she's off limits.* He took several deep breaths, and when he felt in control of his emotions, picked up the tray and returned to the living room.

Her smile as he entered the room almost undid his composure. She had a beautiful smile. Even her eyes seemed to get in on the action. He put the tray on the coffee table nearer to her, and began busying himself pouring the tea.

"The tea smells great," she said. "What kind is it?"

"Just plain old oolong," he said. "I also have jasmine and chamomile, if you'd prefer something more fragrant."

"No, this is fine." She took the cup from him, again brushing her fingertips against his.

"Cream and sugar?" he asked.

"No, black is fine. I like the unadulterated taste of the tea."

A woman after his own heart, he thought, as he lifted his cup, blew on it gently and took a sip.

"I'm the same, I don't like anything getting between me and my caffeine." He put his cup down. "Now, you said on the phone, that you had something important to tell me."

A flicker of worry crossed her face. She put her cup down.

"There are actually two things I wanted to talk to you about, Ed," she said. "You don't mind if I call you Ed, do you?"

"Not at all."

"Good, I'm Augusta, although, my kid brother always called me Augie, and I kind of like it." She did the fluttering eyelash thing again. "Anyway, the first thing I wanted to tell you is that that policeman, the mean one, I think his name's Wayne or something, he came to the office today, and asked a lot of questions, mostly about you."

"What time was he there?"

"Just before I called you," she said.

Damnation, he must've gone straight there after grilling me. I wonder what I said that he needed to check up on? "What kind of questions did he ask?"

"Things like, how many times had you been in Principal Sotheby's office, of course, I told him that as far as I knew, the only time you'd ever been in it was the day . . . you know."

"Which happens to be true," Ed said. "What else?"

"He kept asking me if it was possible that you knew about the private door in his office."

"Yeah, he asked me about a door, too, but I didn't see another door in that office."

"That's what I told him," she said. "In fact, the only people who knew of the existence of that door before now were, the principal, of course, the contractors who put it in shortly after he took the job, me, and . . ."

"His girlfriends?"

Her face turned red.

"Yes, and I believe the number of people who fit that category is quite large. Principal Sotheby was a . . . very social person."

"He had a lot of . . . girlfriends?"

"Oh my, yes. At least four, counting Helen Wheeler. She's just the most recent. In addition to using the door to avoid having to mingle with the students when he came and went, he used it to sneak his . . . girlfriends in and out. Hmph! As if he thought he was keeping his fooling around some kind of secret. Just about every teacher, and probably a few students, knew what he was doing."

Ed looked long and hard at her, so long that she began to look uncomfortable. "Ed, why are you looking at me like that? Oh, you don't think that I was, that he and I—oh, no. I was his subordinate. I kept his appointments, and ran errands for him. Anything else would've been most inappropriate. I, how could you think such a thing?"

Suddenly, it was Ed who was squirming uncomfortably. "I didn't really think it, Augie, but I had to ask. The police seem to want to believe I killed him, and the only way I can get them off my back is to find out who *did*. I didn't, and don't, think it was you, but in order to do a thorough investigation, I had to make sure. You understand, don't you?"

Her expression was a bit skeptical. "I . . . suppose so. I guess if I was in your situation, I'd probably do the same. So, who do you think did it?"

For reasons he could not explain, he found himself trusting this woman, a woman he hardly knew. "I don't know. There are a few possibilities, and now that I know about this door, I will focus on the people who knew of its existence, present company excepted, of course."

"You don't think Helen did it, do you?"

"No, but I understand he was breaking off their relationship. Unfortunately, that gives her motive. And, as you said, she would've known about the door, so she'd have been able to get in and out without being seen."

"True, but I just don't see Helen doing something like that. She's such a gentle, timid soul."

"Well, if it makes you feel any better, she's not my number one suspect."

"Who does that leave?" She looked relieved.

"At this point, I don't want to prejudice my snooping by exposing the names. When I know more, I'll let you know. You wouldn't happen to have the names of Sotheby's other girlfriends, would you? I'm convinced that the killer is someone who knew about that door."

"I don't have them off the top of my head, but he often sent me out to buy gifts, for cousins, he said. And, I had to have them delivered. I have the receipts with names and addresses in my desk. I can get them to you tomorrow."

"That's great, Augie. I don't know how to thank you for being on my side in this."

"No need to thank me, Ed. I've only known you for a short time, but I know that you're no murderer." She looked at her watch. "Oh my, it's getting late. I should be going home. Can I drop by again?"

"Of course, any time."

"I know, maybe next time, I can invite you to my place. I'm a pretty good cook. I could make dinner."

"That sounds great."

She stood, wringing her hands. Ed stood and walked her to the door, laying his hand gently on her elbow as he did. He could feel her arm trembling, and his own hand was quivering a bit. *Good thing she's going home. This could get out of hand, and it's too soon, way too soon.*

At the door, she stopped and turned, looking up into his eyes.

"Thanks for the drink. You make a nice cup of tea," she said.

"Glad you liked it. I'm looking forward to sampling your cooking."

She started to turn, stopped and put a hand on his chest. "Oh, I almost forgot, there's one more thing I wanted to tell you. I got the strangest call today from Georgia Sotheby, the principal's wife. She wanted to know who her husband had been sneaking around with lately. She said she saw the woman leaving by his private door a few days before he was killed, but she wasn't close enough to identify her. Of course, I told her I had no idea what she was talking about."

Ed grabbed her hand and squeezed, then realizing what he was doing, and the fact that her trembling had increased, he released it.

"You mean, his wife knew he was playing around? And, she knew about his private door?"

"Yes, I forgot, she's also a person who knew about it. Back when he first came to work as principal, she used to bring him his lunch, and she'd use that door because he didn't want people to know the principal was eating a sack lunch."

"Interesting," Ed said. "Very interesting. Augie, I think you might just have given me the information I need to point the police in the right direction. Thanks. I could kiss you for that."

The way her eyes lit up, he instantly regretted his words.

"I wouldn't mind that," she said, holding her head up.

Oh, dang it. Me and my big mouth. What do I do now? After blurting it out like that, he couldn't just say he was joking—he wasn't sure he *had* been joking. But, it was too much, too soon. He compromised by gently holding her shoulders as he kissed her on the cheek. She looked disappointed, but still smiled wanly at him.

"See you soon," he said. "And, if this works out like I think it will, I owe you a special night on the town. The restaurant of your choice."

Again, the lights brightened in her eyes. "I'm looking forward to it."

He stood there in the door until she got to her car parked in his driveway. He waited until she began backing out, and when she waved, he waved back and went back inside, wondering what he was getting himself into.

CHAPTER 17

The next morning, he met Ernesto, Violet, and Rose at the community center dining room for breakfast. After enduring a few minutes of Ernesto ribbing him about his 'date,' he cut him off and told them what he'd learned about the secret door, and about Sotheby's wife not only being on to his philandering, but also that she knew about the door, and had used it in the past.

"Do you think his wife killed him?" Rose asked.

"I don't know," Ed said. "But, since she knew he was having affairs, and about the door to his office, she has to be considered a suspect."

"That's right. The spouse is always the number one suspect," Ernesto said. "So, what're we gonna do about it, Ed?"

"I've been thinking about that. Ordinarily, I'd go talk to her to see if I can get a read on her, but, I've never met her before, so that could backfire. None of us have an excuse to talk to her. So, I'm gonna ask Carl to look into it."

"You sure you don't want one of us to talk to her first?" Violet pointed at herself and then at Rose. "We could say we're there to give our condolences, that way we'd have a reason to visit her house."

Ed popped a sausage into his mouth and chewed as

he considered Violet's idea. After swallowing, he said, "No, I think letting the police do it is better. This woman probably knows all the faculty, and she'll know we're not faculty. She's never met us before, and she's likely to wonder why total strangers are going to the trouble of coming to her house."

Violet shrugged and made a face like someone who has just sucked on a lemon. "Have it your way, but I think Rose and I could get something useful out of her."

"So, what do we do?" Rose asked.

"I'm supposed to get the names of Sotheby's girlfriends today," Ed said. "I need you two to check them out."

Violet's prune-faced look changed to a big smiley face, an unusual look for the usually sour-faced Wertheim sister. "Okay, that's what I'm talking about."

"Now, I think I should go home and call Carl."

Ernesto tapped Ed's forearm. "No need. He just came in."

They looked up to see the rumpled detective coming through the dining facility entrance. He stopped and looked around, then frowned. Ed scanned the room, and saw that Janet Murphy wasn't present, which explained Janzen's frown. He waved at him, and beckoned him over.

With a wan smile, he turned and made his way to their table.

"You guys seen Janet?" Janzen asked.

"She was here when we arrived," Rose said. "Probably in the kitchen or her office. I'm sure she'll be back soon. She hovers over us like a mother hen during mealtimes."

"In the meantime, why don't you grab a cup of coffee and join us," Ed said. "I need to talk to you."

Janzen's gaze swung from Ed to the door past the food line which led to the kitchen and Janet's small office. He rubbed at the dark stubble on his chin, making a rasping sound. Then, he shrugged. "Sure, might as well," he said. "Be right back."

In a few minutes he was back, with a cup of steaming coffee, two pieces of toast, and five sausages. He sat next to Ed, took a sip of coffee, and popped a sausage into his mouth. "O'hay," he said around a mouthful of food. "Whafuwan'?"

"It's about the Sotheby murder," Ed said, getting right to the point. "I think whoever killed him must've come through that private door in his office."

Janzen swallowed quickly and looked at Ed through narrow slits. "How'd you hear about the door?"

"When Jefferson and Wayne interrogated me, they kept asking about it, so I asked Augusta Peabody. The first I heard of it was from your colleagues, but I'm convinced that that's how the killer got in and out."

"They should've handled that little detail with a little more finesse, but essentially you're right. They're pretty sure the killer entered and left through that door."

"Which means it had to be someone who knew of the door's existence," Ed said. "Which, by the way, lets me out. I wasn't aware of it until your buddies mentioned it."

"They're not my buddies." Janzen frowned. "Oh, they're good enough cops, if lacking a little in the imagination department, but, they tend to waste time following dead-end leads."

"Like focusing on me as a suspect in this case?"

"Yeah, like that. Look, Ed, I know you didn't do it. And, I think they're coming around to that same conclusion. But, these guys are slow to change their minds. You've just got to hang in there. By the way, I know I pushed you to get a lawyer, but in retrospect, it was probably good that you didn't. Your coming in alone impressed them—well, Jefferson at least. Wayne's still got you in his sights for some reason."

Ed laughed. "Oh, you know how it is, Carl," he said. "When a crime's been committed, and there's a black man on or near the scene, he's always the first suspect."

Janzen didn't laugh. "That's not funny, Ed, and you know it. Besides, Wayne's black."

"Got nothin' to do with it," Ernesto said. "Change what Ed said to, person of color, and you get the same result, and that attitude, my friend, is shared by a lot of people who wear a badge, no matter what *their* color is."

Janzen looked as if he wanted to argue, then he shrugged. "Okay, I guess I'll have to concede that point. But, I don't think that was the case here. I think it's just because there were no other apparent suspects, and you were first on the scene."

"I can understand that," Ed said. "And, that brings me to what I wanted to talk to you about. Have they looked at the wife?"

Janzen took a nibble from a sausage, savored it in his mouth for a few seconds, and then swallowed. "Considering that the spouse is always a prime suspect, I have to believe they have checked her out.

But, to be honest, I doubt she's at the top of their list. It'd be different if he'd been killed at home, but at his office, well, I don't think anyone saw her at the school that day."

"Ah, but she could've been there without being seen. She knew about that danged extra door in Sotheby's office. Furthermore, she was aware that he was using it to facilitate his extramarital affairs."

Janzen paused, a sausage halfway from the plate to his mouth, and gaped at Ed. He put the sausage back on the plate. "I'm not gonna ask you how you came by that bit of information, 'cause if I knew, I'd have to warn you of the potential consequences of you interfering in an ongoing investigation. Just let me ask you this, how reliable is your information?"

"Pretty reliable," Ed said.

"Shit. Uh, excuse me, ladies," Janzen said. "That kinda puts a different light on the case. I don't think Jefferson and Wayne are aware of either of those bits of information."

"You gonna tell 'em?"

Janzen hesitated. "That might not be such a good idea," he said. "I do that, and I'd have to divulge my source, which would make them instantly suspicious. No, as much as I hate sticking my nose in another cop's case, I think I'll check out Ms. Sotheby myself. If I find out anything incriminating, I'll have to figure out a way to pass it to 'em without involving your name."

"You'll let me know what you find out?"

More hesitation, as Janzen looked from Ed to the sausage, looking conflicted. He stabbed a whole sausage with his fork and crammed it into his mouth, chewing furiously, all the time locking his gaze with

Ed's. Finally, after swallowing, he leaned forward. "Oh well, in for a penny, in for a pound, Okay, Ed, I'll let you know what I find. But, you'd better keep this little investigation of yours way on the down-low. Word gets out what you're doing, and . . . well, just be extra careful, okay."

Ed held his right hand up, giving the three-fingered Boy Scout oath sign. "Scout's honor, I'll be like the breeze," he said. "No, I'll be even more discrete than the breeze. They'll never know I was there."

"You know, Ed," Janzen said, shaking his head. "I don't understand half the things you say."

Ed and Ernesto shared a look. "Younger generation," Ernesto said. "No imagination."

"I blame the schools," Ed said. "They don't make them read the classics anymore, so the creative parts of their brains are underdeveloped."

Janzen looked at Rose and Violet, a pleading expression on his face.

"Don't look at us," Violet said. "We've known them for years, and half the time we don't understand anything they say."

CHAPTER 18

Ernesto and the Wertheim sisters convinced Ed that it would be best if he stayed close to home, and allowed them to get out and sniff the bushes. Within an hour of finishing breakfast, returning home, and cleaning his kitchen for the third time, he was regretting it.

He was just about to say to hell with it and going out to do some of his own snooping when the phone rang. It was Augusta Peabody.

"Hi, Ed," she said. "I have those names we talked about last night."

"Great, let me get a pencil and notepad," he said. Fortunately, he kept both items in the drawer of the end table that held the phone, so within seconds he was ready. "Okay, go ahead."

She gave him three names:

Darlene Johnson, 18699 Mockingbird Lane, Rockville
Alma Gortyn, Apt. 12, 29688 Frederick Lane, Gaithersburg
Laura Pennington, 138 Patterson Way, Silver Spring

It appeared that Sotheby didn't like straying too far from home. All of the addresses were a relatively easy drive from Vernon Heights school. Ed thanked her for the information, accepted her invitation for dinner at her house on the coming Friday night, and hung up.

For a few minutes, he debated whether or not to check the names himself. Deciding that to do so would likely upset his friends, who were under the impression that he'd let them do it, he called Ernesto on his cell phone and gave him the information.

That, of course, left him right where he was before the phone rang; bored out of his skull with nothing to occupy his mind but worry about the case. The kitchen was glistening, so he moved to the living room, and using his recently-purchased Dyson vacuum cleaner, attacked the nonexistent layer of dust there.

After moving the hefty machine over a carpet that didn't need it, he flipped the off switch and, leaving it sitting in the middle of the room, took his yellow legal pad and a pen from the credenza and went into the dining room. He put the pad on the table, sat, and began writing in his precise script:

Who killed Douglas Southeby?

Suspect	Motive	Means	Opportunity (Knew about the door)	
Helen Wheeler	Maybe	Maybe	Yes/Yes	
Thomas Hadley	?	Yes	?/?	
Augusta Peabody	No?	?	Yes/Yes	
William Chertoff	Maybe	?	?/?	
Milton Fish	Yes	?	?/?	
Darlene Johnson	?	?	?/Yes?	
Alma Gortyn	?	?	?/Yes?	

Laura Pennington	?	?	?/Yes?
Georgia Sotheby	Yes	?	?/Yes
Ed Lazenby	No	No	Yes/No

He included his own name at the bottom of the list just to be fair, and should anyone else see the list, they would see that he was keeping a completely open mind on the issue. That, too, was why he kept Augusta, Hadley, and Fish on the list, despite being fairly certain that they weren't guilty. The list was in no particular order. He didn't yet have enough information for that, even though his gut was telling him that the dead man's wife should probably be at the top. He hadn't done that, though, because it would've indicated bias on his part, and at this point, he needed to try and keep his mind completely open. He needed more information. His hope was that Carl Janzen's unofficial inquiry would provide that information.

Would the police, he wondered, have a similar list of potential suspects? How would they go about winnowing it? He didn't have the resources available to them. He would have to do it the old-fashioned way, shoe leather and patience.

The phone rang. He answered. "Lazenby residence," he said.

"Ed, glad I caught you," Janzen's voice came over the line. "I got some news about Georgia Sotheby, and you're not gonna like it."

"Okay, go ahead and tell me. She has an iron-clad alibi, right?"

"Pretty much. She was at the Pretty Baby Spa on Rockville Pike from 8:00 to 11:00. Apparently, she went for the full treatment. Anyway, since the ME puts Sotheby's time of death between 7:30 and the time you discovered the body at 9:00, that lets her off the hook. Sorry it couldn't've been better news."

"No need to apologize," Ed said. "It was a long shot anyway."

"For the record, I thought it was a pretty good call on your part. Too bad about her alibi. You hang in there, though. We're gonna solve this thing."

Yes, we are. "I know you will. Thanks for calling."

When he put the phone back on the hook, he stared at it, as if to erase the last few moments. His best clue had just gotten shredded.

What now?

CHAPTER 19

At lunch time, the four friends gathered at Ed's house to review their activities. The news did nothing to improve Ed's dour mood. Rose offered to prepare sandwiches, and Ernesto volunteered to help her, leaving Ed and Violet sitting in the living room. She'd taken it upon herself to brief him on their morning activities.

"We checked out the three former girlfriends," Violet said. "They've all moved on—one's even married and about to have a baby, and the other two have new boyfriends."

"Darn, no motives for any of them," Ed said.

"Worse, they all have alibis. Alma Gortyn was out of town, and just got back two days ago, Laura Pennington's the pregnant one, and she was at her doctor's all morning because of some complications on the day of the murder, and Darlene Johnson's parents were visiting, and they spent that day touring the museums on the Mall."

"That removes three names from our suspect list, and I think we can eliminate Milton Fish, because he wouldn't have known about that private door."

"We can take Tom Hadley the janitor off as well," Violet said. "He also has an alibi."

"Oh, how so?" Ed asked. "He was on campus at the

time, and I don't recall anyone saying they saw him around the time Sotheby was killed."

"That's because he wasn't on campus at that time. He arrived at school early, around 7:00, and took his tools out to do the pruning around the athletic field, and while he was removing the tools, he noticed that his secret stash of booze was depleted. He then he took off to a liquor store a mile or so up the road from the school to replenish it."

"But, his truck was in the parking lot."

"He walked to the store. I guess he didn't want anyone to notice he was gone."

"How'd you find all this out?"

"Simple really," she said. "I just asked myself, who at a school knows everything that goes on, but is never noticed? Why, the cafeteria lady, of course. She comes in early, to get lunch started, and often stays late to clean up. She overhears all kinds of conversations, and this particular one is quite observant. She's seen Hadley sneaking out to his tool shed for a drink throughout the school day—he drinks vodka, by the way, to prevent a noticeable liquor smell—and, she just happened to be emptying some trash and saw him walk off through the trees toward the street around 7:15 that morning. He came back about twenty minutes before the police arrived."

Ed got his notepad, and began drawing lines through names.

Who killed Douglas Southeby?

Suspect	Motive	Means	Opportunity
			(Knew about the door)
Helen Wheeler	Maybe	Maybe	Yes/Yes
~~Thomas Hadley~~	?	Yes	?/?
Augusta Peabody	No?	?	Yes/Yes
William Chertoff	Maybe	?	?/?
Milton Fish	Yes	?	?/?
~~Darlene Johnson~~	?	?	?/Yes?
~~Alma Gortyn~~	?	?	?/Yes?
~~Laura Pennington~~	?	?	?/Yes?
Georgia Sotheby	Yes	?	?/Yes
Ed Lazenby	No	No	Yes/No

"Why didn't you line through you own name?" she asked.

Good question, thought Ed, a darn good question. "Fairness, I suppose," he said. "I still don't have any way of proving where I was during the entire time frame of his death, so my name has to stay on, even though *I* know I didn't do it."

"Is the same for your sweetie?"

"My what?"

"Augusta Peabody, you airhead," she said. "What? You think I didn't notice how you defended her whenever we mentioned her as a suspect, or that we're unaware that she came to your house the other night . . . and stayed for a long time? I know you think she's innocent, so why is her name still on the list?"

"For the same reason mine is. I think she's innocent, but I can't verify her alibi, so she stays."

"Shouldn't be too hard to verify. She said she was running errands. Just ask where she went, and check to see if she's telling the truth."

He'd actually thought of that, but for some reason had been reluctant to ask her. But, Violet was right. If he was going to do a proper investigation, he'd have to ask.

"All right, next time I talk to her, I will."

She reached over and patted his hand, a rare gesture from a woman who gave new meaning to the term, cold and unfeeling. "Don't worry, Ed," she said. "I trust your judgment, and if you think she's innocent, I'm sure she is. But, wouldn't it be good to *know*?"

"Yeah, you're right, it would be good to know."

After lunch, when the others had gone, Ed took the list out and looked at it again. He was tempted to draw a line through his name, but he wanted to focus on two things; removing Augusta's name, and finding out which one of those remaining was the real killer.

He poured himself a cup of tea and went into the living room. A few sips of tea, and the weight of all that had happened began to press down on him. He put the cup down, took his shoes off, and stretched out on the sofa.

The sound of his doorbell woke him from a sound sleep. He sat up, put on his shoes and went to the door. When he opened it, he came fully, really, totally awake. Augusta Peabody, still dressed in her normal office attire, was standing on his front porch.

"Hi, sorry to drop in unannounced, but I had

something I wanted to say, and it couldn't wait," she said. "Can I come in?"

"Uh, oh, sure. Sorry, I was napping, and my brain's still not fully awake." He stepped aside. "Come on in. Have a seat. The sofa's still nice and warm from my nap. Would you like some tea?" *Dang it, what is it about this woman? Every time I'm around her, I babble like an idiot.*

"A cup of tea would be fine." She sat on the sofa and crossed her legs, pulling her skirt down over her knees primly.

He filled a cup and handed it to her. She blew on it, and took a sip.

Ed picked up his cup and sipped. The tea had turned cold. He put the cup back down and sat next to her on the sofa. "Okay, Augie, what is it you had to tell me?"

She put her cup down and took his hands, holding them up level with her chin. "First, I wanted to say, I understand that you thought of me as a suspect, but I want to assure you that I didn't do it. If you want, you can check with the clerks at the CVS Pharmacy on Georgia Avenue and Costco in Gaithersburg. Between those two places, I was pretty much occupied from about 8:15 until I came back to the office."

Breathing a sigh of relief, Ed squeezed her hands. "I don't have to check," he said. "You wouldn't offer if they couldn't corroborate your story." He was already mentally crossing her off his list. "Just so you know, I never thought you did it."

"I know, and I never thought *you* did either. That's why I wanted to come and tell you that I want to help any way I can to solve this thing."

"I'm not sure that would be—"

"Nonsense, I want to help. So, what can I do?"

He had a flash of an idea. She *could* help. She could approach the one person on his list that he couldn't.

"Would you be willing to talk to Georgia Sotheby? See if you can get an idea of whether she might've wanted to do something to her husband?"

"You mean like, kill him?"

"Yes, that."

"Sure. In fact, I'll drive by her place on my way home tonight. I'll tell her I came to pay my condolences. Then, I'll see if I can ferret out her mood. How's that?"

"Perfect, but you be careful. If she is the killer, she could be dangerous."

"I will, and thanks for caring." She stood, and he followed, still holding hands. "I guess I'd better be going. I don't want to be stopping at the Sotheby house too late."

He released her hands and walked her to the door. As Ed reached to open it, his hand brushed her lower back, just above the swell of her hips. She turned to face him.

"Well, wish me luck," she said. "This is kind of exciting, you know, playing detective." Her eyes glistened. They were standing so close, Ed could smell the flowery aroma of the shampoo she'd used. He felt a tightening sensation in his chest.

"Good luck," he said in a slightly choked voice. "And, I'll remind you again, be careful."

"Don't worry, I will." She reached up and kissed him lightly on the cheek. "Talk to you tomorrow."

She finished opening the door, her hand brushing

against his and sending tremors up his arm.

For a long time after she'd slipped through the door and gone, the sound of her car's engine fading in the distance, Ed just stood there, looking out into the onset of dusk. It was several minutes before he realized how silly he looked, standing in his doorway staring up into the darkening sky.

Charles Ray

CHAPTER 20

The next morning, Ed begged off joining the others for breakfast, opting instead to just have toast and coffee at home. He needed time to himself to mull over the situation, and develop some idea of what his next steps should be.

At 7:45, he was just starting on his second cup of coffee when his phone rang. It was Augusta Peabody. "Ed," she said when he answered. "I went to Georgia Sotheby's house last night to tender my condolences, and I have to tell you, it was the strangest encounter I've ever had."

Ed's 'trouble' antenna went to full-active mode. "What happened?"

"It's not so much what happened as what *didn't* happen. I know the man fooled around, and she knew it, but even so, one would think she'd show some kind of emotion at his having been murdered, but she was as cold as ice. It was as if she didn't even care that he was dead. It gave me the chills just talking to her."

"You didn't say anything to make her think she's being looked at as a suspect, did you?"

"No, and that's the other odd thing. *She* brought up the fact that the police had questioned her, and pointed out that she had an alibi. I mean, I never even brought anything like that up. She just said it, right out of the blue. That's really strange, don't you think?"

Hardly the actions of a bereaved widow, Ed thought. His curiosity was itching, and Georgia Sotheby was inching closer to the top of his suspect list. But, he needed to get a first-hand impression before he made up his mind.

"I agree that it's a strange thing to do," he said. "I wonder, do you think it's possible that I could meet her face to face?"

"You want to give her the third degree?"

He laughed. "No, that's what the police do. I used to think it was only on TV until they hauled me in. No, I was thinking more of discretely asking a few questions to gauge her reactions, and see if I can catch her in a lie."

"It's possible," she said. "I don't think she knows all the faculty, so I could take you by, and introduce you as new faculty member wanting to pay your respects."

"Won't she be a bit suspicious if you show up again?"

"I'll just tell her that when I told the faculty that I'd visited her, they were upset that they didn't get a chance to do it as well, and as the new member of faculty, you were deputized to represent them."

"Augie, I like the way your mind works. You have all the makings of a great amateur detective."

"Why, thank you Ed. I admit, this is all new to me, but it's exciting. Do you do this often?"

"No, just now and then. This is the first time, though, that I had such a personal reason for doing it. When do you think we should visit her?"

"I think it would look less suspicious if we did it

during the lunch hour. That's when teachers take their breaks, so it would be the logical time."

"Sounds good."

"Okay, I'll call and tell her to expect us."

"I'll pick you up in my car at 11:30, and then drop you back at school when we're done."

"I'll be waiting." He heard a lilt of happiness in her voice.

Ed pulled into the faculty parking lot at Vernon Heights at 11:29. Augusta was standing on the sidewalk waiting for him. She waved as he pulled into the empty slot near where she was standing.

He got out and went around to the passenger side of the 4-Runner and opened the door for her. She had to hike up her skirt to negotiate the high step, so he held her elbow and put his free hand on her waist to help her get up into the passenger seat, letting his hand linger a bit even after she was seated.

"Don't forget to fasten your seatbelt," he said as he closed the door.

After he was behind the wheel and buckled up, she gave him the directions to the Sotheby residence, an older community south of the intersection of New Hampshire Avenue and Norbeck Road, west of Burtonsville. Wide, tree-lined streets fronted colonial style houses, each sitting on at least a half-acre wooded lot. The place smelled of money, which made Ed wonder how Sotheby had been able to afford it on a middle school principal's salary.

"Nice, huh?" she asked as if she was reading his mind.

"Yeah, bet it cost him an arm and a leg."

"I think he had family money, or his wife does," she said. "They both have, had, Mercedes-Benz's, and they don't look old, if you know what I mean."

A cascade of thoughts began tumbling through Ed's mind. What if he'd been looking at the case all wrong? Maybe it wasn't about a grudge or jealousy, but was about money? Or, maybe it didn't matter. The man was dead, and someone killed him. The challenge was to find out who.

She pointed to a two-story, red-brick colonial surrounded by stately oak trees just up ahead. "That's their house."

Sotheby's, unlike the other houses, had considerably more than a half-acre lot surrounding it, and the front lawn looked like it had been professionally groomed. That, he thought, had to set him back a pretty penny. With the local lawn service companies charging thirty to forty dollars to mow a tiny yard like his, he couldn't even imagine what Sotheby had paid to get the attention these grounds obviously got. He turned into the driveway and drove up to within a few feet of a two-car garage. He got out and helped Augusta down. They stood there for a few seconds, just looking around and taking it all in.

"Nice," he said.

"Wait until you see inside," she said. "Makes the outside look like a slum."

The walk from the driveway to the front entrance was lined with azalea bushes in full bloom, with shiny, dark green leaves. Black mulch was packed neatly around the roots. The front door was a dark brown wood with a three-paned window at eye-level. The glass was frosted, making it impossible to see more than shadows inside the entryway. He pushed the doorbell button, and heard the sound of classical music echoing from inside.

A tiny, brown-skinned Hispanic woman, wearing a black dress with a white apron, opened the door.

"Yes, may I help you?" she asked in barely-accented English.

"We have an appointment to speak with Mrs. Sotheby," Augusta said. "We're from Vernon Heights Middle School."

The woman stepped aside. "Please, come in." She turned and walked toward a high, arched opening. "Please, have a seat in the living room, and I'll tell the madam you're here."

While the entryway was almost as large as Ed's living room, the living room was huge. It seemed to span the entire half the width of the house, with a spiral staircase at the right, leading to the second floor, and another arched opening to the left, through which they could see a portion of a large dining table. Ed counted six chairs that he could see through the archway. The living room was sparsely furnished, but all of the furnishings looked expensive, and there were original oil paintings spaced about the walls.

Ed whistled. "I see what you mean. Southeby was indeed the lord of the manor."

"Told you."

The sound of heels clicking on wood floors above them drew their attention to the stairwell. A slender woman, appearing to be in her late forties or early fifties, wearing a shimmery one-piece yellow dress that clung to her gaunt figure, was coming down the stairs. She had an oval face, and blonde hair that was pulled back on the sides, and tied in a ponytail at the back. What would've been an attractive face, Ed thought, was marred by the arrogant tilt of head, and the cold look in the icy blue eyes. Her thin lips, painted light red, turned down in a sneer, and as she approached them, she seemed to be looking down at them along her aquiline nose.

"Miss Peabody," the woman said. "You're quite prompt." She looked at Ed, more, she seemed to look *through* him, at something a few feet behind him. "And, you must be the faculty representative."

"Yes, ma'am," he said. "Ed Lazenby. I've come to extend condolences on behalf of the faculty of Vernon Heights. We're so very sorry for your loss. If there's anything we can do for you . . ."

Without offering to shake hands, she walked past Ed toward an ornate sofa, where she sat, crossing her legs. "Thank you for your concern, Mr. Lazenby, but I have Maria here to see to the house, and everything else is taken care of."

Ed studied her carefully. For a woman whose husband was brutally murdered, she seemed just *too* calm and in control.

"Pardon me for asking, Mrs. Sotheby," he said. "But, do you know anyone who would want to harm your husband?"

Her face changed; only for a fraction of a second, but Ed caught it. She shot him a look of pure venom, before allowing the aloof expression to resume. "Of course not," she said. "Douglas was respected by his peers, and his staff. I suppose there might be a few parents who didn't care much for him, given that he ran an academically strict school, and he could be something of a disciplinarian, but I seriously doubt that any of them would resort to murder just because their little darlings got detention or held back, do you?"

Funny, he thought. Most people would be curious at a total stranger asking such a question, but she seemed to just brush it off. Something was definitely off about her. But, she had that damned alibi.

"I suppose you're right," he said. "But, someone was upset enough at him to kill him. It just seems strange, him being just a school principal, I mean. It's not like he's a big-time gambler or politician."

"Bad things happen, Mr. Lazenby. Why are you so curious about it, anyway? Are you like those people who slow down near the scene of accidents, in hopes of seeing a little blood and gore?"

"Oh, no, ma'am. I'm just sort of an amateur detective, and this case has me puzzled."

"Isn't it the job of the police to investigate this case?"

"Well, yes, of course it is. But, well, look, I'm sorry. I shouldn't have asked such an insensitive question. Just forget I ever did, okay?"

She gave him a dismissive look, as if to say, 'I've already forgotten it, and you as well.

Augusta tapped his arm. "I think maybe we should go now, Ed, and let Mrs. Sotheby have some privacy."

"Yes," the woman said from her place on the sofa. "I would like to be alone right now, if you don't mind." She stood, and headed for the stairs. "Thank you very much for coming. I assume that you can find your own way out."

They watched as, with her back straight, she

ascended the stairs, never looking back. They had been royally dismissed.

Outside and in the car, Ed blew a puff of air in frustration.

Augusta touched his shoulder. "I told you she was strange, didn't I?'

"You certainly did, but I wasn't sure what you meant until I saw her myself. That woman' has a heart of ice. She's capable of killing someone, of that I have no doubt, but she has that alibi."

"You mean the spa?"

"Yeah, according to my friend at the police department, she was there almost the entire morning. She checked in early, before Sotheby was killed, and checked out well afterwards."

"Checked in and checked out," she said. "And, the police are assuming that means she was there for the entire time?"

"Well, of course, that what that means."

"They didn't get someone to swear that they saw her there the entire time?"

"I don't know, I assume . . . oh, my goodness," Ed said. "You're right. The way they put it to me, they checked the time she arrived and the time she left. I know Carl Janzen well, if someone had told him she was there the whole time, he would've said that. He's a bit more thorough than those two colleagues of his. I imagine when they got the times, they just moved on."

"So, you know what we have to do now, don't you?"

"I know what I have to do. Really, Augie, I shouldn't be involving you in this anymore."

"You're not shutting me out now, Ed Lazenby," she said. "I haven't had so much excitement in years.

Besides, have you ever been to a spa before?"

"Well, no as a matter of fact. Why?"

"Take it from me, I know the spa she went to. It's for women only, and you'd stick out like a pimple on prom night. I, on the other hand, can go in and blend in. I can get the staff to talk to me. They'd probably call the police if you went in asking questions."

"You're really intent on doing this, aren't you?"

"I am. Now, take me back to the school. I'll drive by the spa after school, and come to your place tonight and let you know what I find out."

"You know, Augusta Peabody, you are one stubborn woman. I'm glad you're on my side."

She smiled, a curiously enigmatic smile that Ed couldn't interpret. "So am I," she said.

Charles Ray

CHAPTER 21

After dropping Augusta back at the school, Ed returned home. When he hadn't heard from her by 5:30, he rousted Ernesto out of his house, and they had a quick supper at the community center, returning to his house by 6:30. There were no voice mails on his phone. Either she hadn't called, or, like many people, didn't like leaving voice messages on answering machines. Nonetheless, it began to worry him.

"Dang it," he said. "Augie should've called by now."

"Augie, is it? So, you two are hittin' it off well," Ernesto said.

Ed explained what they'd done that afternoon, and Augusta's insistence on helping with the investigation by visiting the spa to do a more detailed check of Georgia Sotheby's alibi than he suspected the police did. "She said she was going right after school, so she should've called by now."

"I wouldn't worry. That woman looks like someone who can take care of herself. Say, why don't we call Rose and Violet and get the rundown on what we've learned so far?"

"Good idea." Ed called and issued the invitation.

"They'll be here in about ten minutes. Want a drink?"

"I wouldn't say no to a whiskey."

They were halfway through their first drink when the Wertheim sisters arrived. Violet entered the living room like a force 3 hurricane, tossing her jacket *at* the coat rack near the closet, walking to the sofa, and helping herself to Ed's half-empty whiskey glass. Rose, always the proper one, picked up her older sister's jacket and hung it neatly on the rack, and then joined her sister on the sofa.

"Really, Violet, you should wait until the host offers you a drink, not just help yourself," she said.

"That's okay," Ed said. "If Violet doesn't mind drinking from the glass I've been slobbering in, I certainly don't. Would you like a glass of wine?"

"Yes, if you please." She gave her sister a snotty look.

"I'll have a refill on the whiskey," Violet said.

"Help yourself," Ed said. "You already have, why change now."

Rose and Ernesto were laughing as he went into the kitchen. Violet merely shrugged and picked up the bottle of Jim Beam and refilled Ed's glass. "Better bring another glass for you, while you're out there," she said.

He returned with a bottle of white wine from the refrigerator, a wineglass, and an extra water glass to replace the one that Violet had expropriated. After pouring wine for Rose, he poured whiskey for himself and then lifted his glass in a toast.

"Here's to our success," he said.

"But, we haven't solved the case yet," Violet protested, but toasted and drank anyway.

"I know, I'm just hoping to bring us some good luck by visualizing success," Ed said.

Over the next hour, they discussed the case, and their lack of viable leads, and lowered the level in the bottle of Jim Beam considerably. Even Rose, not usually a heavy drinker, sucked down three glasses of wine—actually, she sipped the first glass and a half, but halfway through the second glass had gotten tipsy enough to start guzzling it. After finishing her third glass, just as the wall clock began chiming 8:00 pm, she decided to 'cut out the middle man' and just drink straight from the bottle. She was saved from spilling wine all over her blouse by the sound of the doorbell.

A bit unsteady on his feet, Ed made his way to the door. He opened it to reveal Augusta Peabody, arms on her hips, smiling broadly.

"You, my dear, will be happy to know that I think I've solved this case," she said. She sniffed. "You've been drinking." Then, as she stepped past him and into the living room, she saw the others. "You've all been drinking."

Rose waved the wine bottle in the air. "Yes, we have, darling, why don't you come and join us."

Augusta frowned at Ed.

"Sorry," he said. "We were just celebrating our lack of progress. Come on in and join us. We have wine and whiskey. Which would you prefer?"

"What are you having?" She smiled warmly at him.

"Uh, Violet, Ernesto, and I are having whiskey. Rose's drinking wine."

"I'll have a small whiskey, neat, please," she said.

Ed went to the kitchen and got another glass. He poured two fingers of the amber liquid into it and handed it to her.

Lifting the glass, she said, "I propose a toast to *progress* in this little investigation." She tilted her head back and drained the glass. Then, she handed the empty glass to Ed. "Another, please."

Stunned, Ed complied, pouring until she put her hand on the rim of the glass when it was half full. After putting the bottle back on the table, he motioned her to the sofa, and took his chair opposite Ernesto. She squeezed in next to Violet, on the end of the sofa nearest Ed, and after adjusting her skirt, smiled at him. She had what he thought of as a mischievous twinkle in her eyes.

"Okay," he said. "How was your trip to the spa? I was beginning to worry, because it took you so long."

She took a sip of whiskey, a more ladylike sip this time, and put her glass on the coffee table.

"I took so long, because I believe in being thorough. I told the woman at check-in that I was a friend of Georgia Sotheby's, and that she'd raved about her last trip, so I wanted the same thing, and, believe me, she got the works, manicure, pedicure, scrub bath and facial. Actually, it's quite refreshing."

"I bet it's expensive," Violet said, slurring a bit from the whiskey.

"It's not cheap, but worth it. In more ways than one, actually, because in addition to refreshing my tired muscles, it rips Georgia's alibi to shreds."

Everyone leaned forward. Rose, the less-inebriated of the four, was the first to speak. "How so?" she asked.

"Well, it starts with the scrub bath. They take you to a private room that has a sunken tub that contains some icky-looking green liquid. They claim it's extract of dill, apple, and sage, or something, and that it helps to rehydrate your skin and makes it possible to easily scrub off dead skin. It smells kind of icky, too, but that's not the real important point. Anyway, the important point is, they take you to this room, tell you to disrobe and slide into the tub, and then they leave."

"I suppose that makes sense," Ed said. "Some people don't like taking their clothes off in front of others, even those of the same gender."

"Yes, but they don't come back for ninety minutes," she said.

It took a few seconds for the import of what she was saying to penetrate Ed's whiskey-fogged mind. "What? You mean you were alone for an hour and a half?"

"Maybe even a bit longer. They make allowance for the time it takes you to undress, spend ninety minutes in the bath, and then get out and rinse that green goop off and put on a robe."

"Is there a way to get out of the place without being seen?"

"There certainly is. The rooms with the baths are in a private area off to the side, and there's a door that exits onto the parking lot. It opens easily from both sides, so you could slip out, and back in, and none of the staff would be the wiser."

"Darn," Ed said. "That means that she *could've* been at the school around the time they think Sotheby was killed. But, no, if she killed him, she would've gotten blood on her clothing. Surely, someone at the spa would've noticed that."

"Not if she had a change of clothes in the big gym bag she carried."

Ed looked at her quizzically.

"That's right," she said. "The girl on duty said she had this large gym bag. She only remembered it, because she's a regular, and she'd never come with one before."

"Well, that kinda cinches it," Ernesto said. "She had motive, and now we know she had the opportunity. We oughta take that to Carl and insist that they pull her in for questioning."

Ed shook his head. "It's good evidence," he said. "But, not compelling. All we have is the possibility that she could've sneaked out of the spa. We need some more hard evidence before the police will do anything. Don't forget, because those two detectives consider me a suspect, anything I tell them will be . . . suspect."

Violet tittered. "How on earth can you be making puns, and a lousy one at that, at a time like this?"

"It wasn't a pun, at least, not intentionally. Besides, if I don't laugh, I might cry." Ed shrugged.

"So," Ernesto said. "What do we do now?"

"I suppose we might as well finish this whiskey," he said.

Everyone but Augusta, who begged off, stating that she needed to be semi-sober to drive home—and, she gave Ed a strange look when she said that—joined in the task of finishing the bottle of Jim Beam. By the time he herded everyone out the door, did Augusta linger a few moments longer in the door than necessary, he thought, he was unable to stand without swaying dangerously, and even in his inebriated state, he knew that he would wake up with a whale of a headache the next morning.

CHAPTER 22

Ed hated it when he was right about unpleasant things. And, when that unpleasant thing he was right about was a hangover that made his mouth feel like a stretch of the Mojave Desert, with the sound of a symphony's drum section pounding in his head, and with double vision thrown in for good measure, he really, really, really hated it.

He was only glad that he hadn't vomited up the light supper he'd eaten—as if not upchucking was an achievement to brag about.

Morning came way too early. The lances of light spearing through the gaps in his bedroom curtains sliced into his eyes like hot pokers, and even the sound of his bare feet on the carpet was too loud. The phone rang as he was gingerly making his way to the bathroom, it's bell sounding like it was inside his head and set on the highest volume.

His day was starting on a decidedly sour note.

"Hello," he said, with a growl in his voice. "This better be important, because I need to go to the bathroom bad."

"Yeah, I know, I got a hangover, too," Ernesto said. "Of course, prob'ly not as bad as yours from the rude way you answered the phone."

"Definitely not as bad as mine. Now, what do you

want, I really do need to pee."

"I just called to say maybe we oughta skip breakfast at the community center this morning, seein's how you don't sound too chipper, and I imagine Rose and Violet are in worse shape. You know, at the end, even Rose was drinkin' whiskey."

Ed didn't remember that. There were a number of things he couldn't recall about the evening. For some reason, though, he still remembered that look Augusta had given him when she left.

"Sounds fine to me," he said. "Not sure I could handle their food this morning anyway. I think I'll just do toast and coffee."

"You could try some hair of the dog that bit you," Ernesto said.

"That's just about the dumbest thing I've ever heard. Drinking when you have a hangover just makes you drunk again, so you don't notice that the hangover's just hanging back to plague you later. No thanks, my friend. I'm swearing off booze for at least a week."

"Yeah, okay. See you at lunch?"

"If I'm still alive." Ed broke the connection without saying goodbye. He was feeling too miserable to worry about being polite, even to his best friend.

After relieving his bladder, he stripped and took a long shower, alternating the hot and cold water, which helped to relieve some of the aches in his body, and brought his headache down to a tolerable level. He brushed his teeth, which helped the dry mouth and horrible aftertaste, but skipped shaving, because his hands were still a bit shaky, and he didn't trust them even with his safety razor. At times like this, he wished he didn't have such a thing about electric razors. He'd tried one, and hadn't been satisfied with the closeness of the shave, but at least, he wouldn't've had to worry about slicing his throat with one.

Feeling as if he might survive, he dressed in slippers—no socks—brown chino pants, and a beige polo shirt, and went to the kitchen.

The growling of his stomach caused him to turn away from the bread pantry. His body needed something more substantial if it was to fully recover from the night's debauchery in a reasonable time. He had a real hankering for a few slices of bacon with hash browns, but wasn't sure he'd be able to stand the grease. Instead, he sliced sour medium-thickness slabs off a smoked ham from the meat hamper, heated a skillet and rubbed a bit of vegetable oil over the hot surface. He then dropped the slices of ham in the skillet and put it on the stove set on medium heat. It began to sizzle almost immediately, and the smell, which filled the room, made his mouth water. Simple toast wouldn't do with the ham, so he rubbed some butter on two slices of bread, sprinkled on a little cinnamon and sugar, and put them on in the oven. The sweet smell of cinnamon joined the woody aroma of the frying ham. While the ham and toast cooked, he ground some beans from the canister containing his Jamaican stash, and put them in the percolator, and set it to perking. The kitchen was soon filled with a mixture of aromas, all designed to entice the taste buds. He was almost able to forget his hangover.

When everything was done to his satisfaction; the ham just slightly browned on both sides, the toast nice and brown, with little bubbles of sugar-coated cinnamon dotting the surface, and the coffee a rich, dark brown, he filled cup and plate and took them into the living room, where he sat at the end of the table and dug in.

His meal finished, and his headache now totally gone, he felt better. Good enough, in fact, to wash his dishes and scrub his sink.

He looked at his watch. It was 8:45. A bit later than his usual breakfast, but considering his condition upon awakening, not bad. He was now ready to face the day.

He'd been thinking as he ate, and had come to the conclusion that Georgia Sotheby had killed her husband. He couldn't have told anyone how or why he'd become so certain, it was just the way his brain worked. Facts just fell into place. He could even guess how she did it.

After checking in at the spa, and being left alone in the scrub bath, she'd redressed, sneaked out the back, and driven to the vicinity of the school; probably parking near the same place he and Ernesto had parked when they were conducting their covert recon of Thomas Hadley. She'd then walked to the school, a journey that would've taken her past the tool shed, where she couldn't possibly have failed to notice the unsecured tools. She'd taken the pruning shears, maybe concealing them in her gym bag, and entered her husband's office through the private door. He would've been surprised at her unannounced appearance, but probably not overly worried, unless he had an assignation planned, though Ed doubted the man would do something like that so early in the day. After killing her husband, she'd probably left through the same door, walked back to her car, and returned to the spa, where everyone thought she'd been all the time.

It was a pretty good scenario, and one that he was sure wasn't too far off the mark. He was missing one thing, though. While she might have a motive, her husband's infidelities, why had she waited so long to do it? Was it planned, or committed in a flash of anger? Her taking the pruning shears indicated premeditation, didn't' it? But, why now? Why not earlier, since the gossip was that the man had been sleeping around for years? And, why the pruning shears? Surely there were better, and less messy, ways to rid oneself of a philandering spouse.

The missing information worried him. Not that it really mattered. He could now point out to the police that, she did in fact have the opportunity, thanks to their slipshod checking on her alibi. She had motive, which would be easy enough to check. He was reaching a bit on the means; it depended on whether or not she'd been near the tool shed that morning, something he couldn't prove.

He saw two things he had to do. The first was to inform the police of the hole in her alibi. Calling Jefferson or Wayne was out; they would probably not believe him. So, he called Carl Janzen.

When he got him on the line, he told him what Augusta had learned.

"That sure shoots the shit out of her alibi," Janzen said. "Damn those two knuckleheads. I bet they just called and when they were told what time she arrived and what time she left, wrote that down and didn't ask any more questions. By the way, how'd you find that out."

"I sent someone to use the same service she got," Ed said. "That's how I found out there was a window of time when she could've left the place." He decided to leave Augusta's name out of it, just in case things backfired.

"Well, I'm gonna have a little talk with Jefferson and Wayne. They got some more work to do, and maybe a little apologizing."

"No apology necessary. I just want to see the truth come out. There is one thing that bothers me, though; why'd she wait so long to do it? I hear he'd been playing around for years."

"Who knows? Maybe she finally just got tired of it, assuming that she's the one who did it. Now that we know her alibi sucks, we'll put the pressure on. The truth will come out."

"I know," Ed said. "Just curious. You know how I am."

"Yeah, I do." There was silence for what seemed to Ed to be far longer than Janzen's usual pauses between sentences. "Ed, you're not planning to do something foolish, are you?"

Yup, he'd paused far too long. "Me, do something foolish? Why would you ask that?"

"Because I know you, and I know you can't keep your nose out of a mystery. I also know you're hiding something from me."

"What am I hiding?"

"Stop playing innocent, Ed. You keep repeating my questions, and that tells me you're hiding something." Another pause. "Hey, you're not planning to take a run at this Georgia Sotheby yourself, are you?"

"I assure you, Carl, that I have no intention of interfering with the police investigation."

Janzen made a growling sound. "You're one sneaky old bastard, you know that. You manage to avoid answering my questions, no matter what. Well, listen to me, and listen good; don't go near Georgia Sotheby. You could mess up the investigation, or worse, if she *is* the killer, you could be putting yourself in danger."

"I have no desire to put myself in danger," Ed said.

Janzen growled again.

"You and those wacky friends of yours are gonna be the death of me yet."

"You have a nice day, Carl. I'll let you know if I hear anything else."

Janzen mumbled something unintelligible and broke the connection.

"I think I'll take a little ride," Ed said to the wall.

Charles Ray

CHAPTER 23

He'd wrestled for a long time with whether or not to call ahead and ask for an appointment to speak with her, but decided that Georgia Sotheby, if indeed she'd killed her husband, wouldn't necessarily want to talk to anyone from his place of work, or anyone else for that matter. Besides, he reckoned that showing up unannounced just might throw her off guard enough that she'd slip up and say something incriminating.

That was his hope, and he kept reminding himself of the possibility as he drove across Montgomery County to the housing estate where she lived.

By the time he pulled into her driveway, right up to the garage door, and turned off his engine, he'd just about convinced himself that he'd be able to pull off what he knew Carl Janzen would call a batshit crazy stunt.

The same maid answered the doorbell, and gave him a curious look through narrowed slits, a look that was not friendly. "What you want?" she asked, and her tone was definitely not welcoming.

"I'd like to speak with Mrs. Sotheby," Ed said. "It's a matter of utmost urgency."

She stepped back just enough to allow him to enter, but interposed her body in a way that sent a clear signal that he was not to proceed further until he'd been accepted by the mistress of the house. Then, she buttressed that impression by saying, "You wait here. I go tell the madam."

She turned and walked toward the living room, her boy-like hips swaying beneath the black dress she wore.

A few minutes later she was back with an aloof look on her nut-brown face. "She say you can come in, but just for a few minutes. She's waiting for you in the living room."

He followed her to the cavernous living room. Georgia Sotheby, dressed now in a beige, flowing gown that hugged her slender figure, sat on the large sofa, a flute of champagne in her hand, and an open bottle in an ice bucket on the kidney-shaped, black iron coffee table. She looked up with a condescending expression when Ed entered. He stopped in front of her, and the maid kept going, past the staircase, toward the back of the house.

"What do you want, Mr. Lazenby?" Her tone said she didn't really want to know.

She neither offered him a drink, nor asked him to have a seat, so he decided to play her game. He moved to the leather chair that was catty-corner to the end of the sofa where she was sitting, and sat, crossing his legs, and placing his hands on his knee.

"I'd like to talk to you about your husband's murder," he said, getting right to the point, and noticing that she blinked when he said the word 'murder.' "There are a number of things about it that don't make any sense."

"Why should that be of concern to you? Aren't the police investigating it?"

Now, he thought, was time for a bit of misdirection. "Well, this might come as a shock to you, but, even though I only knew your husband for a very short time, only a couple of days in fact, the police seemed for a time to think that I was a suspect."

Her eyebrows did a little dance, a micro-expression that most people would've missed, but Ed was a trained observer, and he'd been watching her face closely. The momentary look on her face was one of surprise, where he would've expected to see shock, or even fear.

"Why would the police think you killed him?" she asked.

"He and I had an argument, a minor disagreement, really, a couple of days before he was killed, and someone overheard and told the police. My sense is, they were so desperate to find someone close to him with a motive, they picked up on it and ran with it. Of course, they now realize their error, and are focusing on a much better suspect." He put his left hand over his right and crossed the fingers of that hand, hoping his lie was not to transparent.

She didn't seem to notice, in fact, except for the momentary flicker when he'd mentioned murder, didn't seem to be paying him much attention at all. Instead, she took a sip of champagne and leaned forward, exposing her cleavage. "So, they no longer suspect you?"

"No, they don't," he lied. "Like I said, they're looking at a much, much better suspect."

This time, only one eyebrow lifted, just a tiny bit, but her curiosity was obvious from thc look in her eyes. "And, just who would that be?"

He hated lying to anyone, even a murder suspect, but now was not the time to expose all his cards. She still hadn't said anything remotely incriminating.

"They didn't say," he said. "I just overheard part of a conversation. Just between you and me, though, I don't think the two detectives in charge of this case are particularly competent."

"I have to agree with you there." For the first time, she smiled. "They're certainly more Keystone Kops than Hawaii Five-Oh."

Ed returned her smile. "In my case, for instance, at first, they completely ignored the fact that there wasn't a drop of blood on me or my clothing, which would've been impossible if I'd stabbed him. There was blood spattered on the desk, so it would've been impossible for the killer not to get some on herself."

She stopped smiling. "You said 'her;' do they think his killer was a woman?"

"Oh, that was just a figure of speech." He kept his face impassive. "There's so much political correctness these days, I try to avoid using masculine pronouns as much as possible."

"Oh, I see." Her expression relaxed back into an aloofness. "Tell me, Mr. Lazenby, who do you think did it?"

"Like I said, I didn't know your husband all that well, but from what I saw when I walked into his office, whoever killed him was really angry at him."

"And, why do you say that?"

"Those pruning shears were shoved at least five inches into his chest. Do you have any idea how much force it takes to do that? A lot, I can tell you that. And, that's another thing that puzzles me; why pruning shears? That's not your typical murder weapon."

"If, as you say, it was a crime of passion, maybe they were just handy."

Yeah, handy, Ed thought. The tool shed's on the opposite side of the building from Sotheby's office, so whoever took those shears had decided at that moment to use them—not exactly a sudden flash of anger.

"I suppose so," he said. "I've been trying to figure out who had that much anger at him, and why. I know I asked when I was here last time, and I'm sure the police have asked, but do you know of *anyone* who really harbored that much ill will toward your husband?"

"I've already told you *and* the police that as far as I know, my husband didn't have any enemies." She took another sip of champagne. "Oh, I'm sure he had colleagues who were jealous of his success, but none enough to want to kill him."

Now, it was time to go for the jugular. He knew it could backfire, but her cold, calculated demeanor was beginning to get to him. He wanted to crack through that icy façade of hers, and he thought he knew just the thing that would do it.

"What about jealous boyfriends, or husbands? Do you think any of them would want him dead?"

She paused with the champagne flute touching her lips, and glared at him. It was the first time he'd seen anything other than ice in her gaze.

"Just *what* are you insinuating?" Her words were cold, but he noticed that her hand was trembling just enough to make small waves in the half-filled glass.

"Ah, I'm sorry to broach such an indelicate subject, Mrs. Sotheby," he said. "But, it's common knowledge that your husband . . . played around."

"Are you trying to suggest that my husband cheated on me, sir?"

Her words were forceful, but there was a very slight tremor in her voice.

"Well, he wouldn't be the first man to do just that. In fact, word around the school is that he was having an affair with one of the teachers."

She slammed the glass down on the table so hard, the stem cracked, sloshing champagne over the sleeve of her dress. Her eyes blazed, and her cheeks had turned red. She stood, and pointed toward the exit.

"You, you vile, insufferable creature. How dare you come into my house, and make such an accusation against my husband. Have you no decency? Please leave."

Ed stood, but didn't move away from the chair. There was something about her display of anger that was off. She had the words and actions, but something was missing. He wasn't sure what that something was, but was convinced that she was just putting on an act.

"Come now, you can't tell me that you didn't have your suspicions. Why do you think he had that private door in his office?"

"I said, get out! I will not stand here and listen to such slander."

"I'll go, but, before I do, I'd like to leave you with just one thought. The police didn't do a very thorough job in verifying your alibi, you know. But, they'll realize it, and go back and recheck. And, what do you think they'll find?"

She moved around the table toward him, her hands clawing at him. "I said, get out! If you don't leave, I'll call the police and have you arrested."

"On what charge? I rang the bell, and was admitted. I've not touched you, or anything of yours other than the chair I sat on. I'm sure people saw me arrive, so you'd have a hard time convincing the police that I forced my way in."

She was only inches away from him now, her clawed fingers aiming for his eyes.

"You, son of a bitch. I'll claw your eyes out."

Now, he was sure she *wasn't* acting. She was royally pissed, and when she said she'd claw his eyes out, he had no doubt she meant it. And then, it hit him. There was a certain quality of her voice that had been lacking before, a heat in the tone that was now there, that had only come out when he insinuated that *she* was still a suspect, and that her alibi might be scrutinized more closely. He also saw it in her eyes. A combination of anger and . . . fear. He'd come to push her buttons, and while he had nothing that he could take to the police, he'd seen enough to convince him of her guilt. Now, he knew, was the time for a tactical retreat.

Ed slipped to the side and back-pedaled toward the exit. "Okay, okay, I'm leaving. No need to get all huffy."

She stopped, her shoulders slumped, her hands hanging limply at her side, but there was pure hate in the glare she shot at him.

Ed couldn't resist a parting shot. "You'd better be prepared to explain that ninety unobserved minutes at the spa when the police talk to you again."

He was rewarded by a flicker of fear in her

expression that lasted longer this time. He turned and made a hasty exit. As he went through the front door, he looked over his shoulder. She was still standing by the coffee table, glaring at him. The maid was standing off to the side, her mouth opened wide in shock.

He didn't bother buckling his seat belt until he'd backed into the street and headed for the community exit. He hadn't gotten her to say anything incriminating, but the look on her face when he'd mentioned the spa told him everything he wanted to know.

Now, all he had to do was prove it.

CHAPTER 24

On his way home, Ed detoured to the Costco in Gaithersburg to replenish his larder. After getting home, he called Ernesto, Violet, Rose, and at the last minute, Augusta, and invited them for a backyard barbecue.

Augusta arrived five minutes after Ernesto who arrived ten minutes early. Violet and Rose, as usual, came thirty minutes late, just as the steaks were ready to take off the grill.

The five of them crowded around the picnic table Ed had set up in his backyard, and as they ate, he told them about his visit to the Sotheby house.

"So, she threw you out, did she?" Ernesto asked. "Touchy, ain't she?"

"Well, I did sort of hint that I think she killed her husband."

"That was taking a big risk, Ed. If she's really the killer, she might want to get rid of you."

"If I'd stayed, she might've clawed my eyes out," Ed said. "She was pretending to be royally steamed when I mentioned her husband playing around, but got really mad when I mentioned the hole in her alibi. But, the only weapon she had beside her fingernails was a big bottle of champagne, which it looked like she'd drunk about half. Of course, her maid was there, and I don't think she'd do anything with a witness around."

"I don't know," Augusta said. "A woman who would kill her own husband in cold blood is likely to do anything." She laid a hand on his arm.

Somehow, when they'd arranged themselves at the picnic table, Ed had found himself sandwiched between Augusta and Violet, with Ernesto and Rose opposite him. Augusta had leaned against him at every opportunity, said ooh, and ah, as he related his visit to Georgia Sotheby, and halfway through the evening, had pressed her leg against his and left it there. He found that he didn't want to scoot away, which he wouldn't have been able to do anyway, as Violet had taken up more than half the seat and was sitting with her hip parked against his. Every now and then she'd punch his arm, and when he looked at her, she'd just smile. He was getting uncomfortable, and not completely in a negative way.

"I suppose she would if she could," he said. "But, she's on notice now that the police will be rechecking her alibi, and from the look on her face when I told her, I imagine she knows that they will have some very uncomfortable questions for her."

"I guess this lets you off one hook," Violet said.

"I does—what do you mean, one hook?"

She smiled, with a look in her eyes like a cat about to pounce upon an unsuspecting bird.

"Oh, you know what I mean."

He felt his cheeks getting hot. "I'm afraid I don't," he said. "Would you care to explain?"

"I think I'll just let you find out for yourself," she said, as she reached down into the cooler for another beer.

"Just ignore her, Ed," Rose said. "She's just being . . . Violet."

Ed opened his mouth to speak, but was interrupted by the sound of the phone in his kitchen ringing.

"Excuse me," he said. He rose and went inside.

"Lazenby residence," he said into the mouthpiece.

"Mr. Lazenby," a breathy voice from the earpiece said. "This is Georgia Sotheby. You and I need to talk."

He felt a conflict of emotions. One was worry. The woman was a coldblooded killer, and he had no idea what she might try to do. The other was curiosity. He'd given her a scare, he was sure. Maybe if he went to her house, he'd be in no real danger. Surely, she wouldn't try anything in her own home. His body would be hard to explain, and, there was a chance that the maid lived in. The house was certainly big enough, and Georgia Sotheby struck him as someone who liked to be waited on.

"What have we to talk about, Mrs. Sotheby? You made it very clear this afternoon that you *didn't* want to talk to me."

"I, uh, I've had time to think about what you said. You're right. If they're questioned, the staff at the spa won't be able to say they had their eyes on me for the entire stay. But, I assure you, I never left the place until my treatment was finished."

"I still don't see how that involves me."

"You said that you're some kind of amateur detective," she said. "I'd like to hire you to help me prove I didn't kill my husband."

"And, just how am I supposed to do that?"

"You seem to be quite resourceful. I'm sure that if you put your mind to it, you can come up with something."

He had no intention of helping her prove anything, Had he thought her innocent, he might've considered it, but he was certain that she'd killed her husband. Maybe if he talked to her again, now that she was scared, he might be able to get more out of her.

"Okay, I'll come to your house tomorrow morning."

"No, I need to speak to you right away," she said. "And, not at my house. Should someone see us together, both of us under police suspicion, it might look bad. Can you meet me at the Shady Elm Park? It's on Georgia Avenue, just north of Aspen Hill. Do you know it?"

He vaguely remembered seeing signs for the park when he'd used Georgia Avenue to go into the District or to Silver Spring to see his dentist, and it wasn't that far from PVC.

"Yes, I know it. It's not far from where I live. What time do you want to meet?"

"It's 8:30 now," she said. "Can you meet me there at 10:00?"

That would be long after the park was closed to the public, and it probably was not well lighted. But then, that was probably the reason she chose it. No one was likely to see them. He didn't trust her, though, and he would make sure he didn't get close enough to her for her to use a knife on him, since bladed weapons seemed to be her preference.

"Okay, 10:00 it is."

She hung up without responding. "Well, in for a tuppence, in for a pound," he said to the dial tone.

He hung up and went back outside. When he told the others what had just happened, they all began talking at once, all urging him not to go.

"You should call the police," Rose said.

"I agree," said Augusta.

"And, tell them what? That the dead man's wife wants to meet with me in a park in the dark of night? And, just what do you think they'll make of that?"

"Who cares, man? Let them sort it out," Ernesto said.

While he knew that his friend was right, Ed just couldn't resist it. He was on the scent of an answer to the puzzle of who killed Douglas Southeby, and he *had* to follow that scent. "I'm sure they'll do just that eventually," he said. "But, in the meantime, I'd like to know what's on this woman's mind."

"If you ask me," Ernesto said. "What's on her mind is getting rid of an annoyance by the name of Ed Lazenby."

"I'll be okay. I doubt she'd try to kill me in a public place."

Augusta tugged at his arm. "I wish you wouldn't go."

Violet tapped the opposite arm. "I find myself agreeing with her," she said. "Not, mind you, that you'd be any great loss." Which was as close as she would probably ever come to telling someone she cared for them.

"Hey, you guys just quit worrying, will you. I'll be fine."

The chill that had been cast on the gathering by the phone call, warmed a bit after several more beers. At 9:20, Ed reminded them that he had to go, but invited them to stay on and enjoy themselves, because he figured he'd be back in under an hour, which brought the chill back.

Four worried pairs of eyes watched him as he made his way around the side of the house to the garage.

CHAPTER 25

It only took him five minutes at that time of night to drive to Shady Elm Park. It was on the east side of Georgia Avenue, about equidistant from a housing development to the south and a strip mall to the north. A silver Mercedes S-500 was parked near the back of the gravel-covered lot. That worried Ed. While he wasn't one to blithely stereotype people, most of the people he knew in the area, male and female, had a cavalier attitude about time, and routinely arrived five to fifteen minutes late for appointments. He prided himself in always being a couple of minutes early, so he was surprised that Georgia Sotheby had arrived before him.

He pulled his Toyota in next to the Mercedes and got out. While the parking area was lit, though not very well, by light poles at the four corners, the rest of the park was shrouded in darkness, with the inky-black shadows from the surrounding trees creating obsidian islands, dotting a sea of blackish green. He looked inside the Mercedes, but it was empty. *Now, where in hell could she be?* "Mrs. Sotheby, are you here," he called.

At first, there was no response. Just the whisper of wind through the trees. He began to get an uneasy feeling in his stomach, and felt a tingling sensation at the base of his skull as if there was a spider crawling across his neck. Ed had only ever watched a couple of horror movies in his life, the last one being 'Nightmare on Elm Street,' and he always found it odd that in a life-threatening situation, the characters, rather than doing the smart thing and getting as far away from the situation as possible, always walked into the darkness where the monster awaited them. He'd always told himself that, in a similar situation, he'd run away as fast possible, yet, here he was, walking toward the darkness of the trees.

"Mrs. Sotheby," he called louder. "Where are you?"

When she appeared, at first an inky-black shadow, and then a vague shape in the gloom, he jumped back a foot.

"Holy shit, you scared me," he said. "Excuse my profanity."

"Sorry, I didn't mean to startle you," she said, but she didn't really sound like she was sorry.

"Why are we meeting here in the dark?" he asked.

"As I said on the phone, I think it best that no one sees us meeting."

"Okay, I guess I can understand that, but why here in the dark? There's no one in the parking lot, and it's light enough there for us to see each other."

He heard her sigh, and from the movement of the shadow, thought she must have shrugged. "The reason we're meeting here in the dark, Mr. Lazenby," she said. "Is that I don't want anyone to see me kill you."

Ed stopped ten feet from her, frozen in his tracks. He began to think that coming to meet her wasn't such a good idea after all. He couldn't see what kind of weapon she had to engineer his demise, but hoped that it was a bladed weapon, not a gun.

"W-why on earth would you want to kill me?"

"Simple, Mr. Lazenby. You know too much. I'm assuming, nosy old man that you are, that you've not yet told the police what you know, so the best way to deal with it is to make sure that you never get a chance to do that. You haven't told them anything, have you?"

She stepped forward a few paces, and Ed's heart thumped. In the scant light from the light pole behind him he saw the glint of something in her hand. It didn't look like a knife, in fact, it looked suspiciously like a small automatic pistol. *Damn! I really miscalculated this one. How am I getting out of this pickle?*

"Now, hold on a minute, lady," he said. "If you kill me, that only leaves you as a prime suspect. The police know I've been talking to you, so my death will make them doubly suspicious."

She laughed harshly. "Really? This park's a long way from my house, and I have no reason to ever come here. You, on the other hand, live near here, so when they find your body, they're likely to think you came here to meet someone else, and things went bad. You'll be just another statistic."

He hated to admit it, but he knew that she was right. Despite his age, if he was found shot to death in a deserted park, it was likely to be chalked up to a drug deal gone bad. Sad to say, far too often, when black men of any age were found dead in questionable locales, the police were quick to blame drugs or, maybe in his case, a mugging. This area around Georgia Avenue had a significant Latino population, and that was another group that the police were often quick to suspect of illicit activity. He realized that he'd walked into a no-win situation like a damn fool.

In movies and TV shows, the killer often felt the need to unburden or brag just before killing, and while he knew this seldom happened in real life, he felt an urge to keep her talking, figuring that as long as she was talking, she might not shoot him.

"But, I don't know anything. I've just been guessing. There's really no need to kill me. The police are unlikely to believe it if I try to tell them that you killed your husband. After all, what reason would you have for that?"

"What reason?" Another harsh laugh. "Oh, let me count the ways. That bastard's been spending my money—that's right, we live in that big house, and drive expensive cars because I inherited money from my parents. You don't seriously think he could afford it on what the school system paid him, do you? He had it all, and what did he do? He used my money to find, wine, dine, and screw other women."

"But, he's been doing it a long time. Why kill him now?"

"The bastard started sleeping around as soon as we were back from our honeymoon," she said. "I got used to that. But, I ignored my cousin's advice to do a pre-nup before we were married, and I gave that shit full access to *my* money. Oh, I know he was using it to entertain his honeys, but I could live with that, if it meant he wasn't at home pawing me. But, then, I found out he'd been siphoning money out of our accounts and putting it in a private bank account to which only he had access. That was the last straw.

Playing around's one thing, but stealing my money . . . no fucking way was I going to let him get away with that."

Ed took a step backwards. Her coarse language spelled trouble. Gone was the veneer of sophistication she'd worn at her house. This was a woman bent on murder.

She raised her hand, and shook her head, and Ed saw that it was indeed a small caliber handgun, probably a .22 or .32. He didn't know if she was a good shot or not, but figured the farther away from her he was, given the lack of reliability of aiming a handgun, the more chance there'd be that she'd miss, giving him a chance to duck into the darkness, or make a run for his car. He took a couple more steps.

"Stop right there," she said. "Or I'll empty this clip into you. Chances are, I won't hit a vital organ at first, so it'll really hurt before you die."

He stopped.

"Before you shoot," he said. "Tell me, how did you do it? How'd you manage to get into your husband's office with a pair of pruning shears and not alert him? And, why did you use pruning shears?"

"Hell, you're not going to be telling anyone, so I guess there's no harm in telling you before you die."

He let out the breath he'd been holding. Who would've ever thought that she'd be the one killer willing to talk about her crime? Then again, he sensed that she wanted to unburden her anger on someone, and since she planned to kill him, he was a good receptacle for it.

"You were right, you know," she said. "After they left me in that bath, I took a plastic coat from the big gym bag I was carrying, and slipped out the back. I parked a few blocks from the school and walked through the woods. My original plan was to shoot the bastard, but as I was walking past the tool shed, I saw those nice, sharp pruning shears just sticking up out of that wheelbarrow, and thought, hey, those won't make any noise, and I figured, they'd hurt even more than a bullet, so, since no one was around to see, I took them."

She'd probably come and gone well before Ed and Ernesto's arrival. "But, how did you manage not to alert your husband? I imagine he would've been curious at you showing up in his office with pruning shears in your hand."

"The gym bag, you silly man. They fit perfectly inside. He was a bit surprised to see me, but I gave him a line about missing him, and wanting to make up for the little spat we'd had that morning. I went around behind his desk, and was massaging his shoulders. It got him all horny and excited. Douglas could never resist a woman fondling him. When I had him all relaxed, I took the shears out of the bag, which I had on the floor at my feet, and rammed them into his fucking chest. Then, after taking my blood-spattered raincoat off and putting it into the bag, I got the hell out of there, and made it back to the spa with twenty minutes to spare. My scrub bath was short, but it was the most relaxing one I've ever had."

"I imagine you got rid of the raincoat?"

"And, the gym bag, too. Burned them both in the barbecue on our patio."

"Didn't your maid get suspicious?"

"Maria? No, I sent her shopping before I did it."

"Well, well, it sounds to me like you've committed the perfect crime, well, almost perfect. The police are still gonna be suspicious of your alibi, and I assume you didn't leave prints on the murder weapon?"

"Of course not, silly. I wore gloves. Silk gloves, in fact. Douglas liked it when I massaged his neck wearing silk gloves. I burned them, too."

"So, no prints, and no physical evidence. Even if I went to the police, they probably wouldn't believe me. Without the evidence, they can't really do much to you, so there's really no need to kill me."

She cocked her head to the side. "You might be right, Mr. Lazenby," she said. "But, I don't like loose ends, and you are definitely a loose end. I'm not taking the chance that they won't believe you. If you're dead, you won't be able to tell them." She raised the weapon, and pointed it at him.

Ed tensed, ready to spring to the side, in the hope that it would spoil her aim just long enough to give him the chance to make a run for it, and hoping that at his age, he could still run fast enough and long enough.

She steadied the weapon, holding it in a two-hand stance, which made his heart pound. She'd be less likely to miss than if she tried shooting one-handed.

Just when it looked like her finger was about to tighten on the trigger, a deep voice rang out, "Drop the weapon, Mrs. Sotheby, and get down on the ground, face-down, with your hands behind your head. This is the police, and we've got you covered.?

Bright lights came on behind Ed, illuminating everything in front of him, including Georgia Sotheby, who vainly held her hand in front of her eyes to block the glare. The park was lit up almost as bright as day.

"Mrs. Sotheby, I'll tell you one more time." Ed recognized Carl Janzen's voice. "Drop the gun and get down, or I *will* shoot you."

She tossed the gun to the ground in front of her and dropped to her knees, raising her hands to shoulder level. "Oh, officer, I'm so glad you're here. This man was threatening me. I managed to get his gun and was holding him here so I could call 911."

Janzen came up on Ed's right. Jefferson and Wayne, accompanied by two uniformed Montgomery Police officers, on the left. Janzen stopped. The other four kept moving toward Georgia, who looked puzzled when the first uniformed officer to reach her, pulled her arms down and began putting cuffs on her wrists. She tried to keep them from putting the cuffs on, but one officer held her still while the other snapped them around her wrists.

"You okay, Ed?" Janzen asked.

"Y-yeah, thanks to you guys," Ed said, finally taking in air. "I wasn't threatening her. She invited me here to kill me."

"I know, old friend." He laid a hand on Ed's shoulder. "We had a parabolic mike on you most of the time, long enough to hear her confess to killing her husband." He turned to her. "You hear that, Mrs. Sotheby? We heard everything you said to Ed, how you killed your husband, and was about to kill him. Officer, read her her rights."

The officer holding her elbow pulled a card from his shirt pocket, and held it up to the light. "You have the right to remain silent. You have the right to have an attorney present when being questioned. If you give up the right to remain silent, anything you say can and will be held against you in a court of law. If you cannot afford an attorney, one will be appointed for you. Do you understand these rights?"

She nodded, glaring at him. "Yes, I understand, and I want to call my lawyer."

As the four cops and their prisoner drew alongside Ed and Janzen, she lunged at Ed. "You, bastard," she said, spittle flying from her mouth. "You set me up. I should've known."

"Come on, lady," Wayne said. "What was it about 'the right to remain silent' that you didn't understand?"

Jefferson smiled weakly at Ed and Janzen. "Get her in the cruiser guys, and take her to the station for booking. You okay, Mr. Lazenby?"

Ed nodded. "I'm fine, now. I wasn't so sure a few minutes ago. Mind telling me how you guys knew to be here?"

"It's a long story, Ed," Janzen said. "But, before I tell you, I think detectives Jefferson and Wayne have something they want to say."

Charles Ray

CHAPTER 26

The two detectives stopped. "Okay, guys," Jefferson said to the two uniforms. "Take her in and book her. We'll be in later to formally interrogate her." The officers saluted and, taking their prisoner by the arms, led her to the squad car.

Jefferson and Wayne stood with their shoulders slumped, the expressions on their faces like the expressions of schoolboys who've been caught smoking behind the gym.

"Come on, guys," Janzen said. "You know what you've got to do."

"Mr. Lazenby," Jefferson said. "My partner and I owe you one hell of a big apology. We . . . also owe you a vote of thanks. It was your snooping that helped break this case. I'm curious, though, what made you check on whether or not she was seen the whole time she was at the spa?"

"I didn't really think of it," Ed said. "A lady friend of mine mentioned what happened at the spa; you know, how things work. So, after we talked about it, she went and asked for the same treatment Mrs. Sotheby got, and that's how we found out that she was unobserved for up to ninety minutes, more than enough time to get from the spa to the school and back without anyone seeing her."

"Well, that's some pretty good investigating anyway.

My hat's off to you."

Wayne, who had remained silent, with a somewhat sullen look, finally looked Ed in the eyes. Some of his sullen expression faded.

"I really acted like a shit, man," he said. "All I can say is, I'm sorry. I was way off the mark on this one."

As a young man, Ed had been taught that one of the marks of a gentleman and a civilized man was the ability to forgive. It never did anyone any good to hold grudges, and, in a way, he understood why Wayne and Jefferson had done what they did.

"I understand," he said. "No harm, no foul. Besides, I owe you gentlemen for arriving like the cavalry, and saving my life, for that lady would surely have killed me if you hadn't."

"Oh, I don't know," Jefferson said. "You strike me as an enterprising sort who would've figured a way out of the mess you were in."

"After all," Wayne added. "You found the holes in her alibi . . . although, we would've eventually figured it out, you know."

Ed laughed. "I knew you would, which is why Mrs. Sotheby wanted me dead. You see, I told her that you would eventually figure out that she had the opportunity to kill her husband."

"Dammit, Ed, why would you do a dumb thing like that?" Janzen shook his head. "You're lucky she didn't kill you on the spot when you dropped that bit of news on her."

"I don't think she would've tried anything at her house. In addition to the fact that her maid would've been a witness who would also have to be disposed of, I don't think she would countenance getting blood on her fine furnishings. Besides, there's the problem of what she would've done with my body."

"Okay, that makes sense. No, instead, she'd lure you to some isolated spot, and do it there, where there'd be no connection to her." Janzen continued to shake his head. "Why the hell did you accept her invitation?"

"Curiosity, I suppose. Now, tell me, how did you know I was here?"

"Oh, that. Fortunately, your friends are wiser than you are. As soon as he left your house, Ernesto called me and told me where you were going, and who you were gonna meet. So, I got these two, some gear, and a couple of patrolmen and followed you. We picked you up as soon as you turned onto Georgia Avenue."

"Well, you certainly did a good job of that," Ed said. "I never saw you."

"We might be slow checking alibis, but we do know how to do vehicular surveillance," Wayne said. "By the way, good job, getting her to confess. We got it all on tape. The DA's gonna love this."

"Again, Mr. Lazenby," Jefferson said. "Accept our apologies for what we put you through."

Janzen slapped Ed's shoulder. "Now, go home and get some sleep, and please try to stay out of trouble for at least a week or so."

Ed held his right hand up in the three-fingered Boy Scout oath. "Scout's honor. I don't plan on leaving PVC to do anything but shop for groceries for the next month."

Janzen shook his head. "Now, why is it that I don't believe you?"

"Is he really that bad?" Wayne asked.

"No," Janzen said. "He's a hell of a lot worse."

As Ed was driving away from the park, the three detectives were still staring at him. As he thought about what he'd just gone through, he decided that he *would* try to curb his natural curiosity for at least a week, maybe two.

CHAPTER 27

Ed kept his promise to Janzen, and himself, for a week. He puttered around his house, played a few rounds of golf with Ernesto, and had afternoon tea with Violet and Rose.

At the end of the following week, he was bored out of his skull. At 4:50, Friday, he was sitting on his sofa, thinking about what he could do to relieve the tedium, when the phone rang.

It was Augusta Peabody.

"Hey, Augie," he said. "How's it going?"

"You didn't call all week," she said. She sounded peeved.

"Uh, I'm sorry. I guess I was just decompressing after almost getting shot."

"You owe me a dinner, remember?"

"Oh, my goodness," he said. "That's right. I'm so sorry, Augie, in all the hub-bub, I forgot. How about tonight?"

"That would be great." The peevishness was gone from her voice. "Where are we going?"

"If you'll recall, I said that you could pick the place."

"Do you like Thai food?"

"As a matter of fact, it's one of my favorite cuisines," he said.

"There's a nice Thai restaurant in Germantown,

right near city center, they have this curried noodle soup that I just love."

"You mean *kao soi*? I love it, too. And, I happen to know the place, Sabai Sabai Simply Thai. It's across the street from the library."

"Why am I not surprised? Ed Lazenby, you are an amazing man. Is there no limit to your ability?" She chuckled. It was throaty, and gave Ed a warm feeling.

"I visited Thailand several times when I was in the army," he said. "So, I'm familiar with the food, and I developed a taste for it. What time should I pick you up?"

"I live on Viers Mill Road, not far from downtown Rockville." She gave him the address. "I like to eat supper early, say around 6:30, so if you pick me up at 6:00, we should be able to make it."

Ed was familiar with the area, easy to get to from PVC, and from there to downtown Germantown, even with evening traffic, shouldn't be more than 25 minutes. "Just to be on the safe side, I'll be at your place by 5:45," he said.

"I'll be ready," she said, and hung up.

He wondered if he'd heard her put emphasis on the last word, and then decided that it was just his ears playing tricks on him. Nonetheless, for the rest of the day, he didn't feel bored.

She was true to her word. When he pulled into her driveway at 5:42, she immediately opened her front door and walked briskly to his car. Without waiting for him to get out and help her in, she opened the door and pulled herself up into the passenger seat. "I like a man who is punctual," she said, as she fastened her seat belt. "And, I'm starving."

She kept up a bit of chatter for the entire thirty-five-minute drive, west on Viers Mill through Rockville Town Center to I-270. Ed took I-270 north, staying in the local lane to avoid the last of the rush-hour traffic, exited at Middlebrook Road and drove west to Century Boulevard, the main thoroughfare running southwest to northeast through Germantown. Despite the hour, he was able to find a parking place half a block from the entrance to Sabai Sabai, and this time, Augusta waited for him to open the door and help her out.

The restaurant was crowded, mostly office workers from the banks, law firms, and other office buildings that were beginning to sprout in Germantown like mushrooms, but they were able to get a table near the front.

Bowing to his experience, Augusta allowed Ed to order for the both of them, only insisting that whatever he ordered included a bowl of chicken *kao soi*. He ordered two large bowls of the spicy, curried noodles, with sides of pork *satay*, and fried curry puffs, and two glasses of Thai iced coffee.

Their food was set before them within five minutes, and without ceremony, they fell to eating. Augusta's cheeks turned red with her first mouthful of the tangy noodle soup, but she smiled, blinked back tears, and kept pace with Ed, who was shoveling his soup into his mouth with gusto.

Thai food and its consumption doesn't encourage dinner table conversation. The very act of maneuvering noodles into your mouth with a combination of chopsticks and spoon, or wrestling a piece of marinated pork covered with peanut sauce off a pointed stick, makes it difficult to focus on anything else. Added to that, the mélange of flavors and textures is itself so engrossing that talk seems meaningless. So, they ate in silence. It was only after finishing the last of the *kao soi* and sweet coffee that Augusta resumed talking.

"That was delicious," she said. "I've never been to Thailand, but every time I eat at a Thai restaurant, I promise myself that one day I will go."

"It's a bit messy politically right now," Ed said. He kept up with what was happening in the world, especially those places he'd been to, more out of habit than nostalgia. "The army took over a few years ago, and they still haven't elected a new civilian government."

"Ooh, that must've hurt the tourist trade."

He shook his head. "Surprisingly, it didn't really. Tourists who were there when the army staged their coup, weren't molested, and many of them thought it was rather interesting. People took pictures of the soldiers, and weren't stopped or molested. The army might like to meddle in politics, but they're careful not to mess with the economy, and tourism is one of their biggest money-makers. Europeans, especially, still flock there in droves."

"So, it's still a great place for a vacation?"

"I guess so," he said. "I just have this thing about military governments. They make me nervous. The army belongs in the barracks, not in parliament."

"You sound like a real Cold warrior, Ed. How long were you in the army?"

"Twenty years, and after I got out, I worked at the Pentagon until I was eligible for civil service retirement. I retired the year I moved into Potomac

Valley Community. Anyway, that's ancient history. What say we go down the street to the ice cream place and splurge on dessert."

"Sounds sweet to me," she said.

Ed paid the bill, leaving a healthy tip. It was still light outside when they exited the restaurant, but a few cars were already driving with lights. A cool breeze blew up the sidewalk from the south, and Augusta tucked her arm in his and leaned in until her head rested against his shoulder as they walked the block and a half to the ice cream shop.

It was still early, and there was only one other customer, so they were served right away, each getting a double-scoop cup, with Ed getting strawberry and mango, and Augusta opting for butter pecan and chocolate.

"It's nice out," Ed said. "Let's take our ice cream and eat in the plaza."

She again tucked her free arm in his and nodded. They walked back north to a little plaza, with three wrought iron tables, each with four chairs, all empty of customers. They sat at the table directly behind a marble planter containing a lush, deep green plant that Ed didn't recognize, and ate their ice cream. Unlike Thai food, ice cream eating can be a noisy affair. They started with sharing each other's treats, resulting in both getting ice cream smeared on noses and cheeks, and lots of laughing.

Once the ice cream was gone, and their faces wiped with a handkerchief from Augusta's purse, they returned to Ed's car. As he pulled away from the curb for the journey back to her house, Augusta laid a hand softly on Ed's right arm, gently so as not to interfere

Charles Ray

with his driving, but he could feel the heat from her palm through his shirt. It felt good.

CHAPTER 28

"It's still early," she said. "Would you like to stop at my place for a while. I have whiskey. I'm not sure if it's the brand you prefer. I also have some beer, but it's domestic, not imported."

"Sounds fine. As for the beer, doesn't matter to me if it's domestic, as long as it's not light. Light beer is like polluted water."

"It's Coor's."

"Love it," he said.

She smiled, and even though it was a bit awkward, she leaned in until her head was again touching his shoulder. Ed felt his face contort into a smile.

She was silent for the rest of the ride, and didn't move her head from his shoulder until he stopped the car in her driveway. She waited for him to come around to help her out, and 'stumbled' getting down from the seat, causing her to fall onto him. She threw her arms around his neck, and for a moment, their cheeks brushed against each other.

"Oops, pardon my clumsiness," she said, smiling.

Ed returned the smile. "No harm done," he said.

Inside her small, but tastefully furnished living room, she removed the light sweater she'd worn over a one-piece green, sleeveless dress, and tossed it over the back of a chair.

"So, what'll it be, beer or whiskey?"

"I have to drive home," Ed said. "So, I'd better make

it beer."

She stopped in front of him, just inches away, and looked up at him. "You don't have to drive home tonight, you know."

He opened his mouth, but at first, no sound came out. He felt as if his brain had suddenly disconnected from his vocal chords. "Uh, oh . . . Augie, are you sure that's a good idea?" he was finally able to ask.

She moved in closer. He could feel the heat from her body.

"I think it's a wonderful idea," she said in a husky voice. "Unless you find me undesirable, that is." She had a question in her eyes.

"No, no, it's not that. It's just . . . well, I haven't had a lot of experience with, I mean, since my wife died, I—"

She put a finger on his lips. "Nor have I, not since my divorce five years ago. You're the first man I've even given a second look at since my ex bailed on me."

"I, I'm not sure I even remember what to do," he said.

She cupped his face in her hands, and pulled his head down, brushing her lips lightly against his. "Oh, I think between the two of us, we can figure out what to do."

Books by this author:

Al Pennyback mysteries
Color Me Dead
Memorial to the Dead
Deadline
Dead, White, and Blue
A Good Day to Die
The Day the Music Died
Die, Sinner
Deadly Intentions
Death by Design
Till Death Do Us Part
Deadly Dose
Dead Man's Cove
Dead Men Don't Answer
Deadly Paradise
Kiss of Death
Death in White Satin
Death and Taxis
Deadbeat
A Deadly Wind Blows
Death Wish
Deadly Vendetta
A Time to Kill, A Time to Die
Dead Ringer
Death of Innocence
Dead Reckoning
Murder on the Menu
Over My Dead Body
Bad Girls Don't Die

The Buffalo Soldier series:
Buffalo Soldier: Trial by Fire
Buffalo Soldier: Homecoming
Buffalo Soldier: Incident at Cactus Junction
Buffalo Soldier: Peacekeepers

Charles Ray

Buffalo Soldier: Renegade
Buffalo Soldier: Escort Duty
Buffalo Soldier: Battle at Dead Man's Gulch
Buffalo Soldier: Yosemite
Buffalo Soldier: Comanchero
Buffalo Soldier: Range War
Buffalo Soldier: Mob Justice
Buffalo Soldier: Chasing Ghosts
Buffalo Soldier: The Piano
Buffalo Soldier: Family Feud

Ed Lazenby mysteries
Butterfly Effect
Coriolis Effect
The Cat in the Hatbox
Negative Side Effects
Murder is as Easy as ABC

Other fiction
Angel on His Shoulder
She's No Angel
Child of the Flame
Pip's Revenge
Wallace in Underland
Further Adventures of Wallace in Underland
Dead Letter and Other Tales
The White Dragons
The Dragon's Lair
Dragon Slayer
The Last Gunfighters
The Culling
*Frontier Justice: Bass Reeves, Deputy
  U.S. Marshal*
Angel on His Shoulder-Revised Edition
Battle at the Galactic Junkyard
Mountain Man
Devil's Lake

Wagons West: Daniel's Journey (from Outlaws Pub.)
Wagons West: Trinity (from Outlaws Pub.)
Vixen

Nonfiction

*Things I Learned from My Grandmother About
 Leadership and Life*
*Taking Charge: Effective Leadership for the
 Twenty-first Century*
Grab the Brass ring
*African Places: A Photographic Journey
 Through Zimbabwe and southern Africa*
A Portrait of Africa
There's Always a Plan B
*In the Line of Fire: American Diplomats in
 the Trenches*
Advice for the Insecure Writer
Looking at Life Through My Lens
Ethical Dilemmas and the Practice of Diplomacy
Making America Grate Again

Children's books

The Yak and the Yeti
Samantha and the Bully
Molly Learns to Share
Where is Teddy?
Catie and Mister Hop-Hop
Tommy Learns to Count
Catie Goes to School

Charles Ray

ABOUT THE AUTHOR

Charles Ray served 30 years in the Foreign Service (from 1982 to 2012), after completing a 20-year career in the U.S. Army. His first Foreign Service assignment was as a consular officer at the U.S. Consulate General in Guangzhou, China. He then served as the sole consular officer at the newly-opened consulate general in Shenyang, China, where he achieved tenure and was reassigned to the Consulate General in Chiang Mai, Thailand, as the administrative officer and acting deputy principal officer.

After three consecutive overseas tours, he returned to Washington where he served as the Special Assistant to the Director of PM Bureau's Office of Defense Trade Controls. After Washington, he went to Freetown, Sierra Leone as Deputy Chief of Mission.

In 1998, he became the first American consul general in Ho Chi Minh City, Vietnam, with consular responsibility for Vietnam from Hue to Phu Quoc Island. In 2002, he became ambassador to Cambodia, serving for three years. During the 2005-2006 academic year he served as diplomat-in-residence at the University of Houston. After leaving that job, he was appointed deputy assistant secretary of defense for Prisoners of War/Missing Personnel Affairs in the Office of the Secretary of Defense, responsible for the recovery, repatriation and identification of personnel missing from World War II to current conflicts.

His final assignment before retiring from the Foreign Service was as ambassador to Zimbabwe, from 2009 to 2012.

He holds a B.S. in business administration from Benedictine College, Atchison, KS; an M.S. in systems management from the University of Southern California; and an M.S. in national security management from the National War College. Ray is also a graduate of the U.S. Army Command and General Staff College (resident/non-resident program), the Army War College's Land Forces Commander Course, and the Defense Intelligence School's Postgraduate Intelligence Course.

His military awards include two Bronze Stars, the Joint Service Commendation Medal, Army Commendation Medal, National Defense Service Medal, Armed Forces Reserve Medal, and the Humanitarian Service Medal among others. He received a Superior Honor and a Meritorious Honor Award from the Department of State, and the Distinguished Civilian Service Award from the Department of Defense.

A native of Texas, Ray now leaves in suburban Maryland, just outside Washington, DC, with his wife, Myung.

www.ingramcontent.com/pod-product-compliance
Lightning Source LLC
Chambersburg PA
CBHW060143130626
46556CB00006B/2469